Swan Dive

Swan Dive

Brenda Hasiuk

Groundwood Books
House of Anansi Press
Toronto / Berkeley

A portion of the proceeds from the sale of this book will be donated to the Post-Conflict Research Center (p-crc.org), which is dedicated to restoring a culture of peace in Sarajevo and other places with a history of conflict.

Groundwood Books / House of Anansi Press
groundwoodbooks.com

We gratefully acknowledge for their financial support of our publishing program the Canada Council for the Arts, the Ontario Arts Council and the Government of Canada.

Financial assistance provided by the Manitoba Arts Council.

Library and Archives Canada Cataloguing in Publication
Hasiuk, Brenda, author
    Swan dive / Brenda Hasiuk.

Issued in print and electronic formats.
ISBN 978-1-77306-146-7 (hardcover).—ISBN 978-1-77306-147-4 (EPUB).—
ISBN 978-1-77306-148-1 (Kindle)

    I. Title.

PS8615.A776S93 2019   jC813'.6   C2018-904185-4
                                               C2018-904186-2

Jacket design by Michael Solomon
Jacket illustration by Natalya Balnova

Groundwood Books is committed to protecting our natural environment. As part of our efforts, the interior of this book is printed on paper that contains 100% post-consumer recycled fibers, is acid-free and is processed chlorine-free.

Printed and bound in Canada

For the people of Sarajevo —
long live your magnificent city.

And for my fellow travelers —
Duncan, Sebastian and Katya —
who loved it there almost as much as I did.

I

August 30, 1999
From: CristElle@hotmail.com
To: Spaho123@hotmail.com
Subject line: WHBS

I need to talk to u ... u owe me that. Mindy won't say your name anymore. She just calls you that WEIRDO HALF-BAKED SHIT or WHBS, which isn't even any shorter.

I know it's my own fault for telling her anything but I'm blaming you anyway.

August 30, 1999
From: CristElle@hotmail.com
To: Spaho123@hotmail.com
Subject line: ignore last message

Forget it. DO NOT fricking answer this message. I meant what I said.

August 31, 1999

I'm writing this because Budgie said I have to. She didn't actually say that — *Laz-Aaar, you have to* — but that's what she meant. She actually said, *You might want to try writing things down, Laz-Aaar. Try telling yourself the story of your life over the past fifteen years.* I told her I'll be sixteen in three months and she pretended not to hear me. *You're the hero of your story, Laz-Aaar. What does that mean to you? What kind of challenges have you faced? What kind of hero do you want to be?*

She throws questions at me one after the other sometimes but says my name slow enough to sound like a movie pirate. I don't even care enough to tell her that name in my file barely belongs to me anymore or that it's pronounced more like *laser,* as in gun.

I know what Elle would say. She'd say it's better than Aidan Snow calling me Crist-Off, as in *Hey, I have an idea for you, Crist-Off. Let's say you fuck off, Crist-Off. Hey, that sounds like some Russian ballet faggot my mom likes. It's Fuck-Off Crist-Off, everyone.*

I was named after my baba's favorite Serb actor, Lazar Ristovski, but then she decided I had weirdly bushy eyebrows for a two-year-old and started calling me Krysztof, after the famous Polish film director, Krysztof Kieślowski. My whole family started calling me that and when I enrolled in school in Canada I decided to go with Cristoff, which I thought was simple enough, but in the end I became just Cris.

I call Dr. Brunotte Budgie because her eyes are bulgy and small, and her nose is kind of beak-like and she wears this green sweater that's so tight you can see the outline of her bra. The old Elle would have said that woman just needs to accept she's no size 4. Most people would probably think she looks okay. Especially if they like budgies.

Writing can be helpful for all of us, she said, *but especially for those who are struggling. Trauma and cancer patients, for instance, often find it very helpful, Laz-Aaar.*

She was the one who said we should wait to talk about the cancer and then went ahead and brought it up right away. Maybe it was her strange birdie way of trying to be nice. Cancer patients, crazies, crazy cancer patients. It was all the same to her.

When *Mi Nismo Andjeli* or *We Are Not Angels* played in the cinema, Mama lost it on Baba Ilić and my sisters for letting me watch such an inappropriate movie for children. I always remember how the Devil kept trying to get Nikola to dump the girl he got pregnant and the Angel kept trying to get him to marry her.

That was just a comedy, but it's like the Devil wants me to get up and walk out on Budgie like an a-hole, and the Angel keeps playing Mama in voiceover. *After all we've been through. Surely, son, after all we've been through. The doctor is being paid. She is a professional. You must try.*

I don't have to see what you write, Budgie said. *No one does. It's your own private story.*

My sister Amina likes to joke about the year 2000 being the end of the world. She says something called the Bethlehem Prophecies is predicting an epidemic that will kill everything on earth. Tata and I told her the new millennium isn't until 2001 but who knows. When you divide 2000 by 3 using integer arithmetic you get 666, the number of the Antichrist.

So in a few months maybe I'll be saved.

September 2, 1999

When you think of your childhood in Sarajevo before the war, what do you think of?

This is the kind of pointless question Budgie asks. I told her the usual — birthdays, wasting time with my sort-of friend Arman, watching TV after school.

But she wanted details, moments, *memories that still feel alive*, and I tried to look like I was thinking really hard, and Budgie said there was no rush or right answers, which didn't help, but I finally came up with smells.

I told her spicy meat mixed with sweet cream makes feel like I'm back in our old kitchen ready for lunch, kicking the underside of the table until Tata tells me to stop and Mama tells him to let me be, the boy is growing and hungry. Or I catch a whiff of something like old Drina cigarette ashes in an empty soup can and then I'm sitting cross-legged behind the snack counter at the cinema and Baba Ilić is popping a Kakao Krem into my mouth with her nicotine yellow fingertips.

Now and then there's something like the dust of crumbling plaster or somebody burning varnished wood and I want to throw up, which probably isn't exactly normal.

Budgie does not want me to talk about Elle yet. She told me we have to work up to it, kind of like when Elle said I should start with Hana's five-pound weights to get buff for our CD cover. Budgie says maybe I still haven't made my peace with the violence of my early years and we should spend some time there, which is a total waste of time. I don't tell Budgie that, but that's what I think.

Because when I think of Sarajevo, I think of all the normal kid stuff — like my sisters, how they used to argue over who got to take my hand while crossing the street or try out their make-up on me and how I pretended to hate it. All three of them were teenagers when I was still potty training so it was kind of like I had four mothers. If I was sitting at home and said I was cold, someone just didn't get me a sweater. I got hot tea that wasn't too hot. I got slippers. I got hugs. Elle told me once I was the apple of a whole bunch of eyes, which is why I am both a spoiled brat and a pleaser.

All I know is that when I think about my life before Elle, it feels like it's in two parts. From 0 to 9, it's all in slow motion. There's my sisters and Baba and Deda Ilić's cinema and my neighbor Arman and being all carefree-happy-la-la-la.

Then it's like the next year or so are in fast forward. There's the siege and the tunnel and Dajdža Drago and the new apartment in Winnipeg.

And then along comes Elle.

Budgie pointed out that Tata's family was Muslim and Mama's was Serbian Orthodox, like this was news to me. She wanted to know if it was hard on my family, especially during the war. This was obviously a biggie for her because she looked disappointed when I had nothing much to say. It made me wonder what else Mama and Tata have told her, and if maybe they've been meeting behind my back. I told her lots of kids at my old school back in Bosnia had families like that. The war made everyone crazy for a while, which is why we left.

Tell me about your dad, she said, *when you were little.*

I wanted to say why don't you tell me since you seem to know more than I do, but I'm not an a-hole, so I told her my tata, Mirza, was a math teacher in the older grades of the elementary. We walked to school together and we ate lunch together and I had no worries. Lots of the kids called him Matematika Mirza, which Mama thought was disrespectful but I don't think he minded. I told Budgie maybe it was because Tata grew up learning the Qur'an, how everyone should be humble and quiet about their good deeds. He was the first in his family to graduate from a university.

But Mama's parents, my Baba and Deda Ilić, ran a cinema right in the middle of the city, and now and then when I hear something outside kind of like the squeal and rumble of a Sarajevo tram car, I'm right back there. I'm eating Kakao Krem in the lobby and smiling at customers who pat my head and shake cigarette ashes in my hair. I'm taking my middle front row seat even though Baba Ilić says too close is bad for my eyes.

Tata's mama, my Nana Spaho, was really old but Mama called her The Tank behind her back and she'd wrap me in her fat halal butcher's wife arms and call me our blessed little *zakašnjela misao*, or afterthought. But Baba and Deda Ilić knew everyone — Serb, Croat, Muslim, Jewish — and everyone knew them. They were like the movie king and queen of Sarajevo, and I was the prince.

Do you ever think about the war? Budgie wanted to know. *About how it affected your family? About how it affected you?*

I told her I don't remember it much, which is the truth, the whole truth and nothing but the truth. I know she might not believe this if Mama or Amina has already gotten to her, held her wrists tight as handcuffs, explained how their hearts broke right in two when they witnessed their magnificent home come crumbling down around their ears. Amina actually wrote a story for the *Winnipeg*

Free Press about how Sarajevo was the Jerusalem of Europe and how watching all our mosques, cathedrals and synagogues end up at the mercy of homicidal maniacs left her with post-traumatic stress disorder. She says her story won an award because she has *experiential empathy.* Hana and Sara say Amina suffers more from middle-sister syndrome, since everything in her life must be high drama or it's not worth her time.

But surely you must have been frightened at some point, Budgie said. *I remember watching reports of the siege as a young woman. Your street was bombed, Laz-Aaar. Your family was short of food and water. You lost your beloved dog.*

I definitely had not told her about my little dog Sima. I'd never said anything about pets of any kind — not Hana's pet gerbil who ate her own babies, or Sara's pet rabbit that made her and Amina's bedroom smell like pee and newspaper ink, or Elle's pet African dwarf frog who won't stop growing. Mama must have told her.

Sima was old, I told Budgie. He went to live with Baba and Deda Ilić for a while, where it was safer and then his bowel got obstructed from eating a rope. But there was no way I could just stop there, with Sima having a good long life. Budgie talks a lot, but she also waits and stares down at her notes and looks like she might sigh but doesn't. I told her that I was scared sometimes, but it didn't feel real.

I'm pretty sure she wanted me to break down, start banging my head against the wall because I was having flashbacks of exploding windows and sniper shots and dead kids in the street. I could have done it, maybe. I could have pulled it off because most days I do feel like slamming my head or punching my own face or slitting my wrists. Only not about any of that.

Elle told me one time that I was the most non-threatening male she'd ever met, and that included her hippie-dippie peace-love-and-understanding dad, Jimmy. Maybe I wasn't cut out for violence except maybe the movie kind, where you can just sit back and enjoy the show. My neighbor in Sarajevo, Arman, was always heading footballs at substitute teachers like it was an accident, or throwing stuff at cats to make them hiss, or punching me hard in the stomach just to say hello, and I wrestled with him now and then so he could get sick of pinning me and then just come over to play cards or watch a movie. Mama said I quit soccer when I was seven not because I was hopeless at hoofing the ball but because I hated all the shoving and tripping and elbows in your face. Amina says only North Americans who don't have a clue about the game call it soccer, but when I call it football here, people look at me like there's no way that kid ever played football.

Maybe Budgie would like this. When we arrived in Winnipeg it was the kind of windy cold that makes your skin feel like screaming, and the whole way to Dajdža Drago's van in the airport car park, Hana wouldn't shut up with her so-so English. She went on and on about how she was the only one old enough to remember our uncle, Mama's beloved younger brother who'd somehow gotten us out of hell and was now taking us to his beee-u-ti-ful home, which she knew was beee-u-ti-ful because she'd seen pictures, and on and on and on until I wanted to punch her in the mouth.

Sitting in the van's heated leather seats, I remember feeling sick because I could actually imagine the blood trickling down Hana's chin and onto her white jean jacket that was no match for Winnipeg at the end of November.

September 7, 1999

Budgie was distracted today by the floods of mucus pouring out her nose.

One time when I had a bad cold, Elle said it was like the Snot River Dam had exploded in my head. She always got mad when I came to school sick because why drag yourself in and infect everyone else when you can stay in bed and take a break from the daily grind?

I bet Budgie is like Hana, the kind who likes to make lists and memorize the rules so she can tell you all about them. Amina says people like that are the first to crack in a siege because the rules don't apply, like a rabbit is your pet one month and dinner the next. Last year Amina told me I'd been oblivious because Mama was so good at faking the rules for me. Like we always had snack at the same time even when the bread was basically cardboard. Or she always told me a story before I went to sleep even if we were in the cellar and there was shelling.

Even Tata did math with me sometimes, especially at the beginning, and the rules in math are always the same.

What I remember most about the siege is feeling bored out of my mind and Amina says that's because I was sheltered and obviously not a very perceptive child. In grade eight, after Mr. Beacon asked if I was being intentionally obtuse, Elle told him I wasn't stupid, I just lived in Crislandia. She said I couldn't help it if I was dreamy and self-absorbed.

Budgie wanted to know what it was like adjusting to a new home. The nose wiping made her look like she'd been pecking away at cherry-colored bird seed. I told her at first Mama refused to look out our windows in Winnipeg, like she was still afraid of being shelled by Chetniks hiding up in the non-existent hills. But she said it was because there was nothing to look at. Back in our flat halfway up the hill in Kovači you could see green grass cemeteries and tile-covered domes and pointy minarets and the old snaking walls of the Yellow and White Fortresses and more terracotta roofs than you could count.

Out our second-floor apartment in St. James there were gray tree branches and cold blue sky. Dajdža Drago said we'd learn to appreciate the clean lines and wide-open spaces of the prairies, but getting used to something and liking it are two different things.

Budgie wrote something down and then asked how I found learning a new language. I told her I came knowing some English because back in Sarajevo, Hana wanted to be a travel guide and so she listened to ESL tapes day and night for two years straight. Mama still goes on about what a tourism mecca the former Yugoslavia was, the only Soviet country where backpackers came to party. But when things went bad and the barricades went up, she was the one who banned the tapes because who in their right mind would want to holiday in our godforsaken graveyard of a region ever again?

After we got to Winnipeg, Amina kept telling Mama that she needed to be patient with Tata, because it's hard to master new syntax and pronunciation when you aren't one for chatter and only speak up when you have something meaningful to say. Even Hana and Sara agreed that it was only natural for a quiet man to grow even quieter in this situation.

He didn't have an Elle saving his bacon by explaining English expressions like *save your bacon.*

Except I wasn't supposed to talk about Elle yet.

What about school? You came to Winnipeg in grade five?

Mama or Tata must have told her some of this, or it must be in some kind of file, so I told her it's funny, if you're watching an American TV show, they would say fifth grade. Everyone in Europe thinks Canadians and Americans are the same, but they're not. Like they say college when Canadians say university. Or they say handbag when Canadians say purse. Sometimes they call a purse a pocketbook. That doesn't even make any sense.

Were you scared to start a new school?

Elle said she remembered seeing me in the halls those first few months and I was *a deer in the headlights, a fish out of water, a ship without a sail*. And I had a geek target on my back.

I told Budgie that school then was kind of a blur, except I don't think she heard me because that's when she ran out of Kleenex and needed to look around her office for some more. The desk, the filing cabinets, the bookshelves — they're all matching coffee brown and she flitted around her little forest of fake wood trying to pretend I couldn't see she finally had to use her sleeve. She had to call her secretary, or whatever you call them now. Elle's mom Mindy works in accounts payable for a furniture manufacturer and Elle says she's very sensitive about titles even though she claims all people are equal no matter who they are or what they do. When Elle calls her a paper-pusher she pretends not to mind, but Elle knows she does, which is why Elle does it. Just like when she calls her Mindy instead of Mom.

What scared you most?

I know the difference between when someone is actually listening and when they're just trying to hold it together.

I maybe wasn't a very perceptive kid but I know fake okey-dokey when I hear it. I asked her if she needed to go home and rest and she said, *Thank you, no, it's just a cold.* Then she started shooting off questions again. *What made it hardest? Relating to kids at school? The teachers' expectations? You mentioned your dad, that he struggled with adjusting. Was that hard on you?*

She acted as if she was asking the same thing as before, like the mucus had clogged up her short-term memory.

I wanted to tell her scary and hard are two different things.

Maybe I should have told Budgie about Dajdža Drago. I know it sounds stupid to be afraid of your own uncle, especially if he's never done anything but help your family, but when he met us at the airport, I was just wearing my school jacket which had gotten way too small and he wrapped his fingers around my biceps and damned to hell those bastards who'd done this to me.

And the thing is, everyone was afraid to tell him I'd always been that skinny.

He enrolled me in an indoor soccer clinic that first month, and I had to get Mama to tell him that I really wanted to play but needed to get my strength back first, with lots of good Canadian milk and grade A eggs. When he took me bowling and every ball rolled into the gutter, I didn't mention that the shoes were too tight and that I felt sick from too much of that cheesy Mexican mess called nachos.

We had to pretend everything was okey-dokey because Dajdža Drago left Bosnia years before the war and Mama called him her lucky star. Mama told his Canadian wife, Sharon, that in high school girls threw themselves at Drago like the harem girls of an Ottoman sultan, but I don't think Sharon minded because her ancestors were a hodgepodge of Icelandic and Ukrainian and Vietnamese, and Hana said if she is not the most beautiful, then she is the most exceptionally attractive dentist in the world.

The first time I told Elle about Dajdža Drago, she laughed her head off. *You're shitting me. You have an Uncle Drago? Sounds like a bad book! Like "After his parents' fatal illness, Cris was shipped off to Uncle Drago's eccentric mansion, where his only companions were a magic suit of armor and a curious rat."*

Elle didn't know Drago actually means *dear one*, and she never met him because we always went to his house, which he built himself and had a walk-out basement and eight-person hot tub. One time after Mama had some plum brandy in the hot tub, she said in Bosnian that it was funny how Tata always thought her little brother was a big talker who went off to find his fortune overseas and now Tata was supporting his family painting apartments in Dajdža Drago's rental blocks. Amina got mad and stuck up for Tata, said everyone knew that Tata was the best math teacher in one of the best primary schools in the country and Mama said she was just joking around and if you couldn't joke with your family then who could you joke with? Tata took his time lighting a cigarette and said even he had to admit that Drago was a force of nature, no more stoppable than an earthquake, and this made Drago laugh and laugh.

One night, though, I overheard Tata say something else to Mama while they were in bed and I got up to go to the bathroom. It was summer, because I remember Dajdža

Drago had barbecued T-bone steaks and then I'd eaten two jam-buster donuts and my stomach was not happy.

Drago says you keep to yourself at work, Mama said in English. *You need to mix with the others, practice your English. How else you going to learn?*

There was no way to see the look on Tata's face, but he answered in Bosnian as usual. *Your brother sucks the air out of the room. I can't breathe, never mind talk.*

There was a long pause. *He's not there all the time*, Mama said. And that's all I remember because I was too busy on the toilet.

September 9, 1999

When I woke up this morning, my head felt like a beach pail full of sand, and I wondered if I just lay there long enough doing nothing, it would loosen up and move into my lungs and pneumonia would eventually take me.

I told Mama I had a cold and I should stay home from the session today and she lost it. *Hana say it's not good for you to stay in here watching the B-H-S movies and playing those T-B games. If you say you can't go back to school right now, you go see doctor. Okay? Okay. End of story.*

She says that all the time now. *End of story.* She must have picked it up at work.

Work is probably why Mama picked up English so much better than Tata. When Sharon said her Filipino tailor was looking for help, Amina said Mama was a high-ranking clerk for the Sarajevo municipal politburo who'd never hemmed a pair of pants in her life. But then just like that Mama was handling the cash in the shop and Sara and Hana were imitating Mama's English with a Filipino accent. *It's your turn to bacuum, Amina.* Or *What's the matter, Krysztof, you look ready to bomit.*

Tata smiled at this sometimes but I'm not sure anyone noticed but me.

So I had to go see Budgie, and first thing she goes ahead and breaks her own rules. Maybe she felt bad that she gave me the plague, or maybe she was just hopped up on goof-balls. Elle taught me that one in grade nine when she was pretty sure Mr. Reimer sniffed coke in the staff bathroom. She got it from her dad who Mindy says is a pothead, which means he smokes marijuana.

So Laz-Aaar, tell me about Elle. How did you two meet?

I told Budgie we met in gymnastics a few months after we arrived in Winnipeg. I didn't tell her the only reason I was in gymnastics was because Mama had started staring at me when I was in my pajama bottoms waiting for girls to get out of the bathroom. She was worried I was getting *bucmast*, or chubbo, thanks to all those dinners at Dajdža Drago's.

The thing is, Mama always joked that she came from a long line of slim and stylish Europeans who would rather chain-smoke than carry a few extra pounds. She said that if her mama hadn't married into a cinema dynasty, she could have been a movie star. And when I think about it, her worrying about us putting on what Elle called *good ol' North American chub* was the first sign that things were going to be okay with Mama. Like for as long as I can remember, she touched up her lipstick after she ate. But once we were in Winnipeg, she didn't do it anymore.

Or she didn't seem to care if Amina chewed her nails. Or if Tata wore Dajdža Drago's cast-off white sweat socks inside the handmade European loafers she bought him before the Chetniks set up a base on the Olympic ski hill.

Then one day she started stalking neighbors at the apartment mailboxes, asking them if they knew any place nearby for her children to get *the exercise*. Then she came home and told us about this wonderful Canadian thing called community clubs. She actually signed Sara up for gymnastics and me for karate and for a while I thought about how I was going to karate chop Aidan Snow who kept talking to me with a cartoon Russian accent. But then it turned out Sara was too old for the program and karate involved a lot of yelling and strange breathing led by a guy who made Dajdža Drago look like a little girl.

The first thing Elle ever said to me was *You go to my school. You're in Ms. Atkinson's class.*

I didn't recognize her at all but I said *Yeah* like it was obvious she would know that about me. I didn't say *yes*, like Amina, but the shortened English Sara was working on. *Good*, instead of *I am fine. Done*, instead of *I am finished. Gotcha*, instead of *I understand.*

Then Elle said, *Somebody told me you have shrapnel in your skull.* I told her I didn't and she said, *I know. People are such liars.*

The only other boy in our gymnastics class was a figure skater who left after the first half hour. Elle told me later that he told her he wouldn't be coming back because he *needed more of a stretch class with more challenge*, which meant we all sucked and he was a competition-obsessed snob. She said with him gone, the only ones left were a giant ectomorph (me), a giant endomorph (her), and a bunch of regular little pussies.

Mama is yelling to me and Tata that it's supper as if we all still eat together instead of just three of us staring at our plates and pretending we didn't wish we were somewhere else.

I told Budgie that later that week I had a hall pass to go to the bathroom and Elle was sitting on the hallway floor outside her classroom. Her legs were spread out like Hana's old Serbian rag doll and she was scraping nail polish off her thumbnail with her teeth. *I laughed too loud,* she said, and I stopped and stared like an idiot. *That's why I'm here,* she said. *I laughed too loud.* I said, *I see*, and walked away, because I really had to go.

I didn't tell Budgie that I remember sitting on the toilet thinking I should have said *oh*, instead of *I see*, or even better, *that sucks*, which I'd just learned from Sara.

I told her Elle came over after the second gymnastics class. We were standing watching the other girls inching across the balance beam because Elle said she'd already had her turn even though she hadn't. She asked me if we had a VHS player, and we did, because Dajdža Drago and Sharon renovated their rec room and gave us their old one. So Elle marched up to Hana, who was on pickup duty even though the community club was only four blocks away from our apartment, and asked if she could come for a play-date after.

Hana looked at me like I had any idea. *A what?* she said in Bosnian. *What does this girl want?* She told Mama later that she thought Elle was asking me out. Eventually Mindy showed up looking the same as always, like she just rolled out of bed and sipping what she called her overpriced, overroasted cup of addiction.

She'd like to visit with your son this afternoon, she said to Hana.

I told Budgie that Elle pretty much talked without stopping from the minute she walked in the door. *My dad says apartments are better because urban sprawl is killing us. But that's just because he can't afford a house and a yard and the whole enchilada. You have a bigger living room but we have a dishwasher. The worst thing about our place is that the elevator smells like feet.*

She said all this while picking through the girls' mess of fake leather heels at the front door or poking at all the wet tights drying on our kitchen chairs like snakes or opening all the mascara tubes I always had to pick up when they rolled off the bathroom counter.

Mindy says it's hell being a woman, which is why I'm not buying in. I refuse to be a victim of my own making.

It turned out her VHS machine was on the fritz so she brought a movie that Mindy had just picked up at Liquidation World for a steal and I tried to pretend I knew what she was talking about. She even brought popcorn, except we didn't have a microwave, which she thought was amazing. I think Sara and Mama had gone for groceries and Hana was pretending to read a textbook at the kitchen table, but Amina and Tata sat down to watch for a while.

Which the one ess Beethoven? Tata asked in English.

The dog, Elle said.

The dog? Tata asked.

That's the joke, I said in Bosnian.

When Mama got home, she asked us if we'd offered Elle some juice or milk or tea and then whacked me and Tata on the back of the head because we hadn't. When Mindy came to pick up Elle an hour late, Mama wouldn't hear of any apologies. *My son has no bisitors very often yet. It good she come, it good she stay.*

It wasn't until they were gone that the claws came out, as Elle would say. Mama wondered why Canadian women thought it was okay to walk around like they were in their pajamas. Then she asked how I could have found this girl at the gym club because she was so *bucmast.*

I told Budgie this meant fat and she said she had to cut our time a little short because she had to pick up her daughter.

—

Back then, Elle was not just *bucmast*. She was *debeo*. And that first day she came over, I was thinking about how to get rid of her before she even left. But it still bothered me, what Mama said. Maybe I didn't know yet that Elle didn't care what anyone thought of her. That she could look after herself.

She says she refuses to be a victim of her own making, I told Mama and the girls.

And they all looked at me like I was talking Swedish.

September 14, 1999

Budgie's partner and their little girl have the plague now. Elle says when people say "partner" they usually mean same-sex, but I doubt it, because Budgie wears a wedding ring and seems the type to say it no matter what. She wasn't snuffling anymore. She just looked like Mama after a night of shelling.

Back in Sarajevo, I hated sleeping in the stinky cellar. Afterwards my ears would ring and one time at breakfast I told Mama that she looked old and she smiled like everything was okey-dokey and Amina said it was just because she had her period. I used to think that getting your period was something like diarrhea, because it gave you cramps and made you spend a lot of time running to the bathroom.

Budgie wanted to know more about Elle and I told her she stopped showing up at gymnastics because she decided that organized activities weren't for her. She said she didn't need to be *so-called instructed by some pimply teen-aged gymnast who was born to be compact and muscular,* and that someone who was a natural had no idea how to teach someone like her, who was not.

After Elle quit, the bendy girls at gymnastics kind of clumped together like I was a lion and they were a herd of antelopes, even though it's the female lion who does the hunting.

But Elle would keep popping up at school, answering questions I hadn't asked her. *Hey, Cris? It's Ms. Atkinson. I heard you say, Mrs. Atkinson. It's Ms. Atkinson.*

Or she'd find me in the cafeteria. *They say people overeat to fill a void but I don't have a void. I just enjoy life. I want it all, baby.*

Or *This taco salad probably has more calories than fries. But I don't care. It's the best thing on the menu.*

I never tried anything on the menu because Mama sent plastic containers filled with noodle soup or beef goulash or sometimes *cevapi* made with store-bought sausage and pita. Or sometimes Elle came by my locker and fiddled with the lock like she might guess the combo. *Jimmy says men who grow up with a lot of women are less hung up on all that macho crap.* I told her that all my sisters talked about was what the dry Winnipeg weather did to their hair or how much they missed so-and-so, who was dead or still living in hell or off in New Zealand where they'd never see them again. Or they had arguments over whose dirty panties were on the floor or how Amina/Hana/Sara could say this or that when she knew damn well it made Amina/Hana/Sara spit nails, and Elle said, *Trust me, Jimmy says you're going to thank them one day.*

Elle acted like it was a given that I would want to hang out with her. *I'm going to my dad's in BC for a month or so. Mindy wants me to take homework this time, but if I don't do it she won't say boo. She sucks at follow-through. So if you're wondering where I am, that's the story.*

While she was gone I actually sort of made friends with a guy called Brandon, who said he was Hungarian but he'd never been to Hungary. He was even skinnier than me and already had pimples on his neck and sat beside me in homeroom. He was always doodling on his math sheets and so I asked him one time what he was drawing, just to make conversation, and it turns out he was crazy for Doom II. He invited me over to play one day, but since I didn't have a game console or a computer, I wasn't very good and I think he was pretty disappointed.

But he didn't totally give up until he got Quest for Glory IV: Shadows of Darkness, which transports you to the Slavic land of Mordavia, where you have to banish the darkness taking over the valley and prevent the summoning of a terrible demon into the world.

I started telling him about the siege, all the worst and gory things I could think of, like how freshly shot people in the street don't look how you might think. Eyes open, still clutching their purse or bread or whatever, they look more surprised than dead for quite a while after. This made him all bug-eyed and impressed, until I had to spend most of the afternoon in the bathroom because I'd eaten too many chocolate-covered peanuts.

Budgie wanted to know if I felt bad I didn't have a game console, which seemed like a dumb question. My birthday is on Canadian Christmas Eve and that year, Dajdža Drago told me to name a present, any present, and I almost asked for a PlayStation or even a Sega, which Brandon said were grossly inferior. But I didn't ask because I knew Tata would have hated it almost as much as he hated his own in-laws in the end.

Tell me more about that game, Budgie said. *Did it bother you?*

This is what happens when you don't watch what you say. You go back to square one. I told her I never found out if I ruined the game for Brandon or made it even better for him, because we never really hung out again.

All I knew was that even though we left, escaped the whole valley of darkness shit-show, somehow it still stuck around my family like a stink.

Budgie made a little *mmmm* sound, like she'd just eaten a yummy piece of chocolate.

I told her I was kind of relieved when Elle came back in March because all I'd got from Dajdža Drago was a hockey stick and practice net that took up half my bedroom.

One day she just appeared again at my locker like she'd never left.

Mindy says I should invite you over to our place.

I said something dumb like, *You're back*, and she leaned in really close to my face.

Nooooo, Cris. It's my ghooooost. I was killed in an aaaaaav-alanche out weeeeest.

Budge said I had a very good episodic memory and I said I'm mostly good at remembering math and stupid things.

I keep thinking about the first time I went to Elle's. It was only about six blocks but Mama wouldn't let me go on my own because it was too cold. *It's nearly Easter, but you freeze your ears in ten seconds.* She was speaking in English because it was Saturday and she wasn't too tired. I asked how her or Tata coming with me in the deep freeze would keep me warmer and she said, *Don't be cleber with me,* and I told her she meant don't be smart with me. And Tata actually spoke up in Bosnian and told me to obey my mother, and besides he wanted to try out the new mittens Dajdža Drago had given them. They were called garbage mitts and they were big and leathery. I remember on the way to Elle's, Tata clapped his hands together and the *boom* made me jump. Our breath was like fog in the clear cold and each clap echoed against the snow banks.

When Elle rang the buzzer to let us up, Tata turned away and said, *You go on now. I'll tell your mother you're safe and sound.*

Elle and I played Monopoly and I kept landing on all the good stuff, collecting $200, buying houses and railroads. She ate round crackers that I learned were called Ritz and that melt in your mouth, and small squares of gouda cheese, and she told me I'd never survive in the real world of capitalism. *Luck only gets you so far. You also need to be cut-throat. You need to be ready to step on the little people and I can tell you wouldn't hurt a fly.*

She was wrong because I'd destroyed plenty of anthills with Arman when we were small, even pulled apart a moth once, and I told her I was trained in karate. She said, *Let me guess, you lasted one class,* and when I didn't say anything she knew she was right and jumped up and down like she'd won the lottery.

I told her she only lasted three gymnastic classes and she said at least she had a philosophy toward life and knew how to walk the walk, and then she explained what walk the walk meant.

Elle took me for my first Slurpee even though it was so cold in March that no one back in Sarajevo would believe it. She wanted to know if I was ever planning to invite her back to my place and I said I didn't know and she aimed her straw at my face and shot blue raspberry Slurpee. She said, *You're such an a-hole,* and then she explained what an a-hole was and said she liked me because I was honest.

Looking back, maybe this would be funny if I didn't feel like my life was over and I will never laugh again.

Amina said the Bethlehem Prophecies also predict that on December 31, 1999, massive solar flares will torch the sky and millions of people will be blinded. So maybe first blind, then dead from the plague because it can't actually work the other way around.

—

When Tata came to pick me up that day, Mindy was at the store buying frozen pizzas.

He was so bundled up I couldn't really see his face but he never said anything about Mindy leaving us on our own. Elle asked him to clap in his garbage mitts like she read our minds and he did and we all laughed like idiots until I could see Tata was starting to sweat in the stuffy apartment doorway.

Before that day I'm not sure I even liked Elle, but maybe instantly liking someone isn't always what adds up to something because after that, we were best friends.

There's something else about Mindy and Elle's apartment. Every inch is covered in stuff because every weekend Mindy goes shopping at Liquidation World and buys a king-size throw pillow or an abdominal crunch bench that's supposed to fold down and slide under the couch or a cafeteria-style food warmer. Elle says she buys a lot as "presents," like the time she brought home an oversized dog basket for her friend's chocolate lab who died before she could give it to them.

I guess that's why Elle always found a reason to come to our place. Sometimes Mindy drove us to a movie or something and she asked about my family, how they were doing, did the girls need her to pick up any great buys on salon shampoo or lilac-scented microwavable heat packs.

I've been making time in the morning to read the stories, she said one time. *When I think of those blackouts, having to cook over a fire in your own kitchen or having to scoop your*

shit into a plastic bag because there's not enough water to flush.
I mean, the least I can do is have you all over for a casserole.
Elle said when Mindy cooked, she was pretty good and
there'd be a whole month of waking up to pumpkin raisin
buns in the bread-maker and coming home to Polish-style
goulash in the slow-cooker.

But there was no way I could invite Mama and my sisters to that apartment. In their kitchen they managed to fit
a table and chairs and water cooler and washer and dryer
and all the blenders and ice-cream makers and waffle irons
that Mindy collected and never bothered to dust or sweep
around. Hana would have faked some kind of stomach bug
rather than eat there and afterwards Mama would make
cleber remarks. *When was the last time that woman read one*
of those recipe books stacked like bricks on top of the kitchen
cupboards? If she takes one from the bottom, the rest tumble
down right on her head.

So we never went there, and I never thought of it until
now. I keep thinking about Elle crowded in there with
Mindy. I'm watching over them like a ghost, wondering
what it must be like to live in such a mess by choice.

September 16, 1999.

Today Budgie was wearing a red shirt with two square pockets right over each *sisa*. She looked like some a-hole dressed up his pet bird in a cowboy shirt. Elle said it's cruel to dress up animals because they're like, *Is this food on my head? Why are you doing this to me, my food-giving friend? Please, if this is not food, I'm not interested.* I told her that when we came to Winnipeg I thought Halloween was just as dumb. You dress up and go out after dark in the freezing cold and people give you candy so you don't trick out their house with eggs and toilet paper? And she said, *So what, the Chinese burn money and cook food for their dead relatives.*

Budgie wanted to know if it was hard to adjust to normal life, especially with Elle and other kids my age, and I told her nobody at my school had any idea about *Dikan* or *Kobra* or any of the other old comics Deda Ilić used to bring me when the electricity went out for good. I read them so much I could act out each panel and it finally drove Amina crazy.

Do you really not have any clue what's going on here? Do you think this is all some kind of game? Do you know that normal guys, like Bog Durić and Miro Popovic, who Hana let feel her up last year, are now murderers? They're hiding up there in Trebevic Mountain, shelling away, and three children younger than you died in a rain of shrapnel today. They don't care if you're Muslim, Serb, Croat or Martian. If you don't agree that being a Serb is more important than your friends, or your family, or your city, they want you D-E-A-D.

Then Mama came down on her for talking about that in front of me, like Amina was as awful as one of the crazy Chetniks who shot little kids.

Or like one day in Sarajevo I woke up to the noise of wheelchairs and old carpets and toboggans being dragged over cobblestone. People used all kinds of stuff to haul jugs of water once the taps went dry, but I just got used to it and fell back to sleep, because what else was I going to do anyway?

Budgie said she read that Bosnians are a fatalistic people because for most of written history they've been in the path of great empires vying for supremacy. I told her she should talk to my sister Amina about that because I wasn't good at history. I was more of a math whiz like Tata.

She told me not to sell myself short, but I didn't think I was.

September 17, 1999

I woke up thinking about that time not long after the grade six talent show, when I slipped on some ice in front of the school and a bunch of crumpled old papers and a container of Mama's white bean soup dumped out. It was just before the morning buzzer and Elle told me no one laughed but no one really came to help either, and she said it was like I was Charlie Brown and she was Lucy. I didn't know what she meant.

You know? Peanuts? she said.

But I didn't know and I asked what was she talking about. *What nuts?*

Forget it, she said, like I was trying to be a jerk or something. *Just let it go, okay?*

And I did, I let it go, maybe because I was used to Elle explaining everything to me and I was too lazy to do it myself. I even saw something about an old Charlie Brown show in the TV guide a few times but I didn't bother tuning in.

So yesterday I asked Budgie what she knew about this Charlie and Lucy and she said they were characters from a comic strip and Charlie had a famously cheeky dog named Soopy. And I asked, *Why Soopy?* and she said, *No, Snoopy.* And I asked, *Why Snoopy?* and she started to look the same way Elle did that morning.

I don't know. Maybe because dogs like to sniff around and get into things.

But Elle said I'm like Charlie and she's like Lucy. Why would she say that?

Budgie said that was a good question, but Elle may be the only person who could answer it. Which was not helpful, so I asked her about Charlie.

I guess he was what you'd call an underdog. He always hoped for the best, but things didn't always turn out.

I asked about Lucy and Budgie rubbed the bridge of her beak. *Lucy thought she knew what was what. She was vain and she liked to … Do you know the expression "push someone's buttons"?*

I told her I knew because Sara said Amina did it to her. *So this was part of the joke?*

Yes.

Were they friends?

She thought about it. *That's a good question.*

I waited, and then she looked at her watch and jumped up because we were eight minutes past our time.

September 21, 1999

I've been going to see Budgie for exactly a month and she's only mentioned the Big C once, which is fine with me, except it's kind of like knowing that someone is going to punch you in the face. Part of you just wants to get it over with. There's no way there's not intelligent life somewhere else in the universe and if I'm lucky maybe aliens will take over the planet sooner rather than later.

One time I tried to explain to Elle about the Zoran Čalić comedy franchise, how in the last movie the two dumb cops meet up with an alien posing as a politician and she said it sounded totally not funny and I told her you had to be Yugoslavian and Sara said she was Yugoslavian and she thought they were the worst movies ever.

Budgie wanted to know what kinds of things Elle and I used to do together as kids and I told her most of the time we obsessed about CristElle. She had no idea what I was talking about, of course.

I said I wasn't even sure how it all started, except Elle liked to say she was a music geek even though she didn't know how to play an instrument or read music or worry if she was a little flat during the bridge. We also watched a lot of videos on TV because when Elle really loves something, like pop moves and pop riffs and pop divas, she really loves something. Like before CristElle, she was really into the TV show *Friends*, so we'd spend a lot of time coming up with our own sitcom plots, like Chandler and Joey are kicked out of their apartment because Joey forgot to pay the rent and they have to move in with Phoebe, who keeps walking around in the buff.

Or Elle went through this thing where she really, really wanted a waterbed because she heard they were good for super-imaginative dreams, so we spent tons of time coming up with ways to earn money, like walking dogs or shoveling driveways. In the end we spent more time thinking up jobs than actually doing any, and whatever we did make went straight to Slurpees, which was good, I guess, because there was no way they were ever getting a double waterbed frame in that apartment.

I told Budgie that one time Elle came back from visiting Jimmy in Vancouver and talking about the buskers in Gastown and how some guy named Aaron who could dislocate both his shoulders had been couch-surfing at Jimmy's. He traveled across North America getting paid to turn himself into a human pretzel. I told Elle that in Sarajevo music students used to sing opera or play violin sonatas for customers in line outside the cinema and she just kept going as if I hadn't said anything. *My point is, you come up with an act, you put out a hat and voilà, a few bucks in your pockets.*

So after that we started blasting Mariah and Janet and Destiny's Child, playing them over and over until we could sing not just the chorus but the entire song straight through.

Budgie wanted to know how we practiced the pop hits at our place with five adults and one teenager all living there. I told her Tata didn't even notice since he was out working for Dajdža Drago all the time, and Mama was her usual self, offering us homemade potato salad or cherry strudel, being all sweet and nice until Elle was gone, when she'd say things to my sisters so I'd overhear. *If she had a voice, she could at least specialize in classical, where fatties are the norm. Shouldn't our boy be outside with other boys doing boy things? Perhaps he was traumatized in ways we cannot see.*

Then Sara and Hana would reassure her because they worried about her blood pressure. *Yes, we know, but give him time. He was never athletic. He's learning English. His marks are fine. Everything will change after puberty.*

The funny thing is, they were right about all of that. Except for the part about Mama not having to worry.

I didn't tell Budgie that. I noticed she likes to suck on the end of her pen, and it kind of looks like she's slurping up a worm.

What did you enjoy about singing?

That was easy. It was the first time I was good at something besides math. And when I started singing American pop with Elle, Amina got all excited. When CristElle was just starting out, Amina was the only one besides me who didn't have a job. She still spent her days writing letters to the *Winnipeg Free Press* about the mortar attack in the city's Markale that killed 68 people, about how many Sarajevo families like ours were of mixed Serb, Croat and Muslim backgrounds, about how mass murderers like General Mladić were getting away with war crimes because the Americans and NATO refused to step in with some serious air power.

One time Elle was reading over Amina's shoulder and she said it might help our cause if those crazy-ass names didn't make you want to give up and read the funnies instead. I thought Amina might lose it on her, like when Elle complained that our apartment smelled like cigarettes because Tata sometimes smoked in the living room with the window open and Amina told her if she didn't like it she could just leave because a man who has lost everything should be able to do what he likes, including perfectly legal if unhealthy habits in his own home.

This time, though, Amina just laughed and squeezed Elle's arm and told her it was our people's fate to be misunderstood.

Maybe she knew deep down that she needed a break from the crusade because for a while it's like she became CristElle's biggest fan. She loved to talk about how I'd inherited my phenomenal musical talent from our artistic Bosnian Serb side. *Our great-grandmother Vanja sang in German cabarets in her youth and her husband Teodor played the piano during silent movies.*

All I know is that CristElle became everything for a while. Elle said we were a team of two, hungry for success, and all we had to do was put in our time, groove ourselves up, master our tunes and then unleash ourselves on the world. *You have to put your heart and soul into it,* Amina told us. *You can't fake that. There is nothing more moving than watching a child put their heart and soul into something.*

Then she told Elle the story about Zlata, the Sarajevo girl who kept a diary during the siege, which was then published by the French and became a bestseller and so her family was released through diplomatic channels.

What about everybody else, Elle wanted to know. *Her family got to go, and the rest of the city is still stuck?*

Amina told her that civil war was like that. Some people lived and some people died and there was no fair or unfair.

I thought it was funny that Elle didn't ask about us. Why were we here in Canada and other families still back there? But the thing about Elle is she's all about the here and now. She doesn't mind if she thinks one thing one week and the opposite thing the next.

I asked Budgie if she ever watched *Star Search*, and she looked blank. *On TV?* I told her, *Yeah, on TV,* and she laughed — a slightly crazy Amina laugh. *Forgive me, Laz-Aaar. I have a toddler, so all I do is wipe bums and not sleep.*

I told her it went off the air in 1995, and she laughed again. *Well, I would have been doing my Master's, so no TV then either.*

Okay, I said. *But it was this show where anybody could go on and do their talent and if the judges liked them, then they got their shot.*

They're shot? she asked.

You know, I said. *Like you win the best vocal group or best comedian and you get a manager and your shot at making it big.*

Budgie's pen was back in her mouth and I wondered if she got this from spending too much time with her kid. I said I never really thought we'd go on *Star Search*. More like it was our inspiration.

Because in the end, we just did the grade six talent contest.

September 23, 1999

I'm trying to remember what else Elle and I did those first couple of years besides plan our rise to stardom. Because there was a lot of stuff besides the actual singing, like designing stages and mapping out tours and thinking about how we were going to spend our millions. We watched a lot of the usual TV, like *Friends* and *ER* and *Party of Five*. And we watched movies after Hana got the job at the post office and bought a new VCR. Amina was the only one who refused to go to the video store because how could she enjoy such indulgence when so many loved ones were still living without electricity?

I didn't bother asking her why VHS tapes were a luxury and not department store make-up because it only wound her up.

I told Budgie that CristElle actually had to go on hiatus for a while because Elle went to her dad's for three months in the middle of grade six. But the truth is she'd been drifting away from the music for a while. Instead of practicing she wanted to spend all our time making videos with the knock-off video camera Mindy picked up at Liquidation World. I asked her what was the point when we didn't even have a recording contract yet, but she had an answer for everything.

Have you ever heard of something called fun? We are now in middle school. Mi-Dull schoooool. Our days of sitting around and being stupid kids and dreaming up fun shit are numbered. As soon as Mindy will sign consent, I'm getting a part-time job so I can buy mics and amps and all the equipment we're going to need. So enjoy this while it lasts.

I tried practicing on my own, but it wasn't the same.

Budgie wanted to know what I did with myself while Elle was gone, and I told her Mama stuck me in swimming lessons, which was not good since I never made it past the shallow end.

Swimming was the worst because even after the lessons were done the water stayed inside my ears, swishing around like there was a kiddie pool in there. I'd be sitting at the kitchen table doing some assignment on the cardiovascular system and there'd be this gurgle every time I turned my head, like the stale pool water was whispering to me, *You can't escape, Cris, you are made of water, we are all made of water.*

Budgie asked how I found doing schoolwork in a second language and I said it was okay, except I never had math homework because the thing I liked best I did the quickest.

Back before the siege, sometimes Tata would throw out matematika problems for me on the way to school and I figured them out all in my head and even though he didn't pat me on the head or put an arm around my shoulder, I always knew this made him happy.

That winter, when Elle was gone and I nearly drowned every Wednesday night, I tried to start this up again and Tata tried to play along. But I could tell he was tired from climbing up and down ladders, and Mama kept nagging him to learn the English numbers and nagging me to teach him, so in the end it wasn't worth the trouble.

Whenever Elle went to Jimmy's for a month or three, it was like putting life on pause. I got up and went to school and went to bed, but nothing ever happened to move the story along.

Budgie wanted to know if I've been writing in this notebook. *Could you share with me the kinds of things you're writing about? No details, but just categories.* I told her I didn't follow. Not to be an a-hole, but because I didn't follow.

Well, let's see. Are you writing about the past, the present, the future?

I thought we were going to talk about the talent contest, I said.

She smiled the same kind of smile that Hana smiles when she's dealing with someone like Mindy.

Okay, let's talk about the talent show. So I told her Elle was still away when I found out about it and I needed to tell someone and Amina was the perfect person because she'd decided that as the youngest child and only grandson, I should also begin a letter-writing campaign to Mama's parents, convincing them to leave Belgrade, the degraded and globally disgraced capital of Serbia, and join us in Winnipeg. Tata actually spoke up then, put a number of sentences together maybe for the first time since we arrived.

They made their choice when they closed the cinema at the first sign of trouble. Ran off to the devil because they could. Now they're safe enough in their soul-dead capital. Besides, your Baba Ilić would find this city too provincial for her tastes.

I told Budgie the contest wasn't just for grade six but the whole school, and first prize was a short-haul WestJet flight for two. Hana wanted to know what kind of school gives children such an expensive prize and I told her the principal's wife works for WestJet and Amina said maybe they want to give the kids some real incentive. Otherwise it would be nothing but lip-syncing and half-baked piano solos. Hana told her it was still ridiculous and Amina asked why she was putting her nose in. Then Hana said, *I thought you spurned such extravagances on behalf of suffering Bosnians,* and Amina said, *Did I hear you right? Are you really accusing me of betraying our people?* And Hana said, *Oh, Christ, Amina. Shut. Up.*

Budgie kept that stupid smile on her face and said she was still waiting to hear about the contest. I told her when Elle got home, she was pumped about it but not as much as I thought she'd be. Jimmy's new girlfriend, Frieda, owned a salon before she moved to Northern BC to become a found-object artist and she gave Elle these tiny little braids she called cornrows. For the first week back, it seemed all Elle wanted to talk about was Frieda and people's hair. *Yours is so thick and wiry, I'm not sure I could do much with gel. Maybe you should shave it down to peach fuzz or something. At least it would be a statement.* Hana always said I was born with a dark shag rug on my head and got out the scissors whenever it passed the tops of my ears. One time, Heath Kamp, who sat behind me in math, slid a chewed-down pencil into my hair. *Observe! The object has disappeared into thin hair!*

It's not thin, I said. *It's thick.*

Whatever, man, he said.

Sara told Mama that it's not good to let me sit around like a vegetable even if I'm doing what Budgie asked, so Mama made me help her make *grah* for supper. I don't remember Mama cooking as much when I was small since she had a good job in a government building and Tata or the girls would often pick up something at the market or the kebab stand on the way home. Now she makes *pljeskavica* and *sarma* and all the things Baba Ilić used to. She says it's because we're on a tight budget but Amina says it's because it reminds her of home. During the siege, Mama first started making *grah* without the meat, and then without the beans, until it was nothing but brown sludge with some rice.

I told Budgie that in the end, CristElle only had the last week of May and the first week of June to prepare for the contest and Elle and I couldn't agree on a song. I wanted to do "Only Wanna Be With You" by Hootie and the Blowfish, but Elle said it was the worst video ever made in the history of humanity. Also there wasn't much of a part for her. She wanted "Candy Rain" by Soul for Real. When Amina suggested "Can't Help Falling in Love" by UB40, Elle said that song was so last year, but Amina said, *Then might as well kiss those plane tickets goodbye,* and even Elle was no match for her because Amina was right. Elle's alto isn't terrible but there's not a lot of range there.

We practiced with Mindy's karaoke machine from the Liquidation World Last Chance Bin and watched the video about a thousand times. Elle let me do the chorus and take the lead, which seemed a little strange because it wasn't like her to give up the spotlight. And she would lose focus over the stupidest thing. Like when Amina brought up the fact that Mama and Tata had been Communists, we pretty much lost a whole hour of a Saturday afternoon.

Seriously? I thought they were Bosnies.

It's Bosnians. But also many *Yugoslavians belonged to the Communist Party.*

Okay, but were they Yugoslavs or Bosnians?

Both. Bosnians, Serbs, Croats, Slovenes, Montenegrens. They were all Yugoslavs. And many Yugoslavs belonged to the Party.

Jimmy would totally love that because he said these days you have to move to the boonies if you want to escape the clutches of capitalism.

Not so in Yugoslavia. Our leader, Tito, was a savvy diplomat and held the different nations together with his own give-and-take Balkan style of social democratic idealism.

Tito sounds like some perverted clown who liked kiddie parties a bit too much.

Only in English. In Yugoslavia, we had a saying, because people were very worried about what would happen to the country after Tito died. We said, After Tito, Tito.

That doesn't make sense.

At that point I kind of lost it because the contest was in five days and this was getting us nowhere. I said, *No, turns out it didn't. Tito's big happy family of Yugoslavia ended up as dysfunctional as they come.*

Elle also kept on about shaving off my "rug." She said Jimmy liked this band called Fine Young Cannibals a few years back and the lead singer had a perfectly buzzed head. I asked her what Fine Young Cannibals had to do with UB40 and she said, *They're British,* like I was an idiot. Of course, once Amina weighed in, it was as good as gone.

First they used scissors, then switched to Tata's electric shaver, and by the time they were done you could have stuffed a pillow with all the trimmings on the floor. Elle even wanted to use a razor so my head would be so shiny it created its own light show on stage and I actually got really mad at her. Like really mad, for the first time. I wanted to know why she kept treating this whole thing like a big joke.

Easy, there, she said. *I think doing lead vocals is going to your head.*

Budgie asked why I thought Elle wasn't as "into the contest" as I expected. She actually made air quotes with her little birdie claws. I told her I didn't know. Elle always dreamed big and maybe a school talent contest was too small potatoes. Maybe it never occurred to her that it was just a stepping stone and those free plane tickets could get us to the *Star Search* set in Orlando. I didn't know then and I still don't. All I know now is that WestJet short-haul flights don't get you to Florida.

Maybe, even all the way back then, I'd already started losing her.

September 26, 1999

I just thought of something. After the girls turned my head into a lumpy peach, Elle said I needed to play sick for two days until the show. *You come out on that stage with your new look and bam, we've got some wow factor. But if they've already seen you, it's old news.*

I told her I didn't want to worry Mama and she said it was just two fricking days because after she got back from Jimmy's that time, fricking became her favorite word. And maybe my family didn't see school like everyone else because after the shelling started, you never really knew if classes would be on or not. Some weeks it would feel almost normal. You put on your backpack and go the usual route, sit in your usual spot, learn the usual things, except Tata and the other teachers weren't always there because things weren't really normal. Some were always missing, especially the ones who'd grown up hunting and knew how to handle a gun. Tata said those poor bastards felt obliged to join the defense forces, with their crappy homemade rifles and crappier ammunition because the UN had basically decided the Sarajevans should be sitting ducks against the entire armory of the former Yugoslav forces based in Belgrade.

Any kind of school days were still the best, though, because you weren't stuck inside watching TV, which sounds good until that's all there is. Or later, when the electricity was off most of the time, playing Žandari with sisters who were so jittery they didn't even care if you could see their cards from across the table.

Or even later, when Arman got hit when he was standing in the schoolyard yelling at some UN white helmets sitting in their truck to grow some balls and give us some guns so it would be a fair fight. I wasn't there, but Amina said the UN soldiers didn't even go get Arman right away, and she didn't know who she hated more, the peacekeepers or the Belgrade-backed lunatics, and Mama told her to shut her stupid mouth and stop upsetting me, then took me in her arms and pointed out that Arman would probably just lose his leg, like this made him the luckiest boy in the world.

After that there was no more school and Mama pretty much kept me as a prisoner.

You show your face at school, Elle said, *and you sentence our wow factor to death.* I told her she didn't understand and she said, *Understand what? You're not going to tell them you have cancer. Just tell them your fricking throat hurts.*

I swear those were her words. And this is what Tata told me the night we left through the tunnel. *I never believed in fate, Krysztof. But this tragedy, this destroyed city, these destroyed lives, it's like some madmen pushed a boulder down the hill and there was no stopping it. Our beautiful Sarajevo was fated to die at the hands of hate and intolerance.*

I was nine. What kind of father tells their kid this and then stops talking altogether? What kind of math teacher believes in fate instead of chance and probabilities?

Maybe that's what war does to you. It makes you superstitious as an old baba. And now it's happening to me too. Because how else do you explain what Elle said way back then like she had some kind of crystal ball?

September 28, 1999

Budgie seemed all wound up today, like she had an itch she couldn't reach. She kept jumping from one thing to another so I reminded her we were talking about the contest.

Elle always said it was a turning point for us, that nothing was really the same afterwards, and Budgie said, *Yeah, the contest, okay, let's finish that up.* I told her I faked sick Wednesday and Thursday and on Friday morning Amina helped me convince Mama I should sleep in so I was fresh to take an exam in the afternoon. The only problem was Amina finally got a job at Robin's donut shop but she called in sick so she could come watch and Hana overheard her so there was a big fight about earning money and loyalty and fingernail clippings on the toilet seat.

Amina told me she didn't care, some things were more important than family unity, so she was there when the whole school gathered in the gym, students on the floor, everybody else in chairs. There was no curtain on the stage but they strung up blue camping tarps on wires and brought in a couple of high school students to do the lights.

I wore a white button-up shirt and black pants that Mama brought home from the tailors because it had been three months and the owner never picked them up. Elle said I looked like a waiter until Amina turned up my collar and they agreed bald Elvis might make a statement. Mindy went to Liquidation World and bought Elle shiny red tights that made her legs look a little like sparkly sausages and an extra-large man's dress shirt. Because she was backup and because of all the brass in the song, Elle talked Mr. Pahl, the band teacher, into lending her a tambourine and a trumpet and a trombone to pretend to play, just like in the video.

We all had to wait backstage, wedged between bins of game pinnies and some cardboard palm trees left over from a pirate play. Elle looked around and decided there were only three real contenders besides us — Natalia Grady, who was in grade seven and supposedly joining the Royal Winnipeg Ballet's professional student program next fall; the band Soulgroan, aka Matt Cohlmeyer, Evan Labun and Darius Khan, who were all in grade eight and huddled together in a corner like the rest of us might be contagious; and Ursa Chipman, who was in my homeroom and went to circus camp last summer.

When Mr. Alexander came on stage there was some problem with the lights so he had to introduce the judges in the dark. There was Mr. Pahl, the band teacher, and Mrs. Dubé, the choir director/librarian, and some lady named Aretha who owned Rising Star Dance Studio and was a friend of our gym teacher. Elle said Muscle-Head Gawronsky was obviously shtooping the dance teacher, which she had to explain to me. I told her I was really nervous and then Mr. Alexander said that the judges' scores would count for half of a performer's mark, and student applause would count for half, and that's when Elle lost it. She sank down into a squat, kind of like a bullfrog in red leggings.

A fricking popularity contest? That's what this is?

The armload of instruments went clanging to the floor, and everyone turned and looked. Even Soulgroan who never looked at anybody.

Budgie asked if I was embarrassed, like when I dropped my backpack in front of the school, and I said no, and I never said I was embarrassed when I dropped my backpack. I told her that maybe Natalia actually didn't look, maybe she was too busy staring at her pink slippers, getting into her dying swan zone. When I first started school, she came up to me in the hallway because she loved the Bolshoi Ballet and thought I was Russian. Amina would have told her we'd rather be dead than backward ruthless Russians who only encouraged Serbia's backward ruthless nation-building, but I just told her I was Bosnian and she looked confused so I told her a Bosnian was someone from Bosnia-Herzegovina, and she said, *Bosni-herzo-where?* I told her again and she said, *Isn't there a war there?* I told her that's why I was here and she said, *Lucky for you, I guess*, and that was it.

Budgie wanted to know if Elle was embarrassed and I told her all I knew was that she was mad because she'd been worrying about the judging since we signed up. A few of the kids in her homeroom had looked at the list and made some snide comments about "really looking forward" to CristElle and I told her lots of people in my class said being famous was one of their top ten life goals so what was the big deal? How was CristElle any different except that we actually had a plan? And she acted like I was the one who said whatever it was they said. *Hello? Are you listening? I don't care what they think. I'm just not their monkey. I just don't want a bunch of little fricking followers to tell me whether I've got the stuff. Most of them wouldn't know talent if it hit them in the face.*

Backstage, she looked like she might throw up. *A fricking popularity contest. Nobody told us this was the deal. This is fricking nonsense.*

I told Budgie I always thought it would be me who'd get stage fright because Elle wasn't afraid of anything, but standing there in the dark wings that smelled of gym sweat and nerve sweat and Natalia's hair gel, I wondered if Elle was ready to walk.

I'd only ever seen ballet from Baba's balcony seats in Sarajevo's National Theatre and watching Natalia it seemed way harder from up close. About halfway through, the music cut out and Natalia kept going like she didn't notice a thing. She just kept floating like a plastic bag in the wind while her feet thumped and squeaked across the stage.

Budgie asked if I still thought Elle wasn't afraid of anything. I said I didn't know, but now I'm thinking I should have said popularity contests.

Mama just got home and she says they need some help at the tailor shop, sweeping up and running errands, and she thinks since I've missed a whole month of grade eleven I should get out of the apartment and contribute to the family.

It's not natural for a healthy Slabic teenage boy to be so pale and solitary.

I pretended I would think about it.

I told Budgie that after Natalia, a kid named Leo played the fiddle and I crouched down beside Elle and I told her we worked so hard and we knew the song and like Amina said, I had the voice and she had the moves. I was the cake and she was the sparkler.

And it worked. Elle rubbed my fuzzy head and hugged me like she was drunk. *I don't care. We're ready. Let's do this.*

And we did, and I can barely remember being on stage except for the light in my eyes and the dark gym floor stretching out like some kind of field growing cross-legged kids. It's like I didn't wake up until it was over and then I couldn't trust my own body, like I might float away into the rafters. I can hear the applause, the hoots and hollers. I can see Elle out of the corner of my eye, breathing so hard and beaming so bright.

And later, there's Mr. Pahl saying we were a delight, that no one had ever sung an Elvis Presley classic in reggae-style quite like that before, and Natalia saying, *Good job, guys, that was fun, that was a total surprise*, and Amina saying I'd stepped into my rightful place as the gifted voice of the family.

Budgie asked if I would sing her a few lines but she didn't give me a chance. *Wise men saaay, ...*

I wanted to tell her that budgies were definitely not songbirds and it was like she read my mind. *You can do better? There's a reason I majored in psychology, not music.*

So I finished the line even though I haven't sung in forever and she kicked her feet in the air like an excited little kid. *You have a very nice voice, Laz-Aaar.*

She wanted to know what happened, if the good guys won, and Amina's voice answered in my head. *Don't be naïve, Herr Doctor. The good guys don't always win. Back then our people were still being picked off by snipers like ducks in a barrel.*

I told Budgie Soulgroan played last and dedicated their song to Kurt Cobain, the artist and the man who had taken his own life just a few short months ago, raging against the machine. I remember Elle calling when she was still in BC to tell me how depressed she was about the news and I told her she didn't even listen to Nirvana and she said, *Correction, you don't even listen to Nirvana. Jimmy says "Smells Like Teen Spirit" will define our generation.*

Budgie wanted to know if Soulgroan were any good and I told her I didn't know. All I knew was that the chorus went, *Get your Gucci something out of my something.*

I never made Budgie laugh before, but this made her laugh. She looked at her watch and asked if I was really going to make her wait until next session to tell me who won, and I said Nana Spaho used to say waiting is good for you. It builds strength. Budgie wanted to know if I thought that was true, and then I laughed because I had no idea, but she was going to have to wait.

September 30, 1999

I woke up thinking of stuff that Elle and I never talked about, or that I never thought about. Like the judges probably marked Soulgroan so high because they played an original song. But should you get extra points for originality if the song isn't very original or very good?

Mama won't stop talking about getting me out of the apartment. I went with Tata to pick up some paint and he kept his eyes straight in front of him pretty much the whole time, like he's afraid to look at the ghost.

Budgie pretended she hadn't been able to eat or sleep since our last session because she wanted to know who won the talent contest and I told her I knew how she felt because the judges took forever to reach a decision. They made all the performers stand up on stage in a huddle and I could make out Amina in the audience, looking like she was about ready to throw herself down, forehead to the floor like Nana Spaho praying in the mosque.

Elle kept whispering to me, *Did you hear them? I think we got the most applause. Seriously.* Natalia stood beside us in her stiff duck-feet pose, pretending not to listen. Matt and Evan and Darius sat with their legs dangling off the edge of the stage, pretending they didn't care what happened.

I told Budgie that when Mrs. Dubé called out CristElle, Elle screamed so loud that my hearing in that ear is still sketchy. We each got a framed certificate and a $50 St. John's Music gift card for coming in third place. Afterwards, Elle said the cheering for us was nearly as loud as for Soulgroan coming second, and Natalia's first place only got your normal polite applause. The truth is I think there were a few boos in the cheering for us, but maybe they were for the judges because the minute we stepped down off the stage, people started swarming us. They said they didn't know I could sing, that they loved that song, that UB40 was the best, that we were the best. Two grade seven boys tried to mimic Elle's pretend reggae trumpet blowing but Amina said they didn't come close to her style. I thought Elle might explode. When she went to hug Amina, her face was red and wet, like she was actually sweating with happiness.

Right after the contest, Mindy took us out for dinner at Boston Pizza which she paid for with half cash, half credit card. Elle ordered appetizers and dessert and non-alcoholic cocktails and Mindy said some things were worth splurging over.

The week after, just before school ended for the year, Mrs. Dubé stopped us in the hallway and introduced me to Mrs. Gulliano. She said she was director of the divisional junior jazz choir and she heard I had a great voice. They practiced Thursdays after school at Westwood United and I should join next year. Elle asked if you had to audition and Mrs. Dubé waved her off. *Cris will blow them away, no problem.*

When they were gone, Elle said that was tacky and I thought she meant like sticky and she had to explain. *Well, like, for instance, couldn't they have waited until I wasn't there to hand-pick you? They acted like I was just your groupie.*

I told her I wasn't going to try out anyway and she asked why not and I said, *What do you mean? Because CristElle comes first,* and Elle said, *Really?* and I said, *Of course.*

Budgie leaned forward like we were going to share a little birdie secret. *Do you think you guys should have won?*

I told her Elle had lots to say about that. *This is what picks my bum. Tons of people have told me that we were the most entertaining and isn't that what it's all about? That trip should have been ours.*

But I have a feeling this wasn't exactly true because Amina was there and if there was some kind of grand injustice she'd have been all over it like a fly on butter.

I just wanted to get back to our regular practicing but Elle said I was being a wet blanket. Like on the last day of school, she ran up all excited because some girl in grade seven whose dad played the bongos wanted to join us and I had to say, *Okay, you really want to change our name to CristElle-Phoebe?*

Budgie laughed again. She said we should probably move on, maybe make it as far as grade seven this session and I couldn't tell if she was being snarky. I know *snarky* because Mindy said she always had to be ready for one of Elle's snark attacks and I wondered if maybe Mama and Tata were running out of money to pay Budgie.

Or maybe head doctors only want you to go on and on about your childhood when it involves war crimes.

I keep thinking about the time we got our first UN package during the siege. Mama talked about it for days before, telling me to just eat the cabbage soup without crackers or the nearly rotten tomato without salt, because very soon we'd have rice, we'd have meat, we'd have treats. And when the container finally came, everyone acted like it was Christmas Eve at Baba and Deda Ilić's, until Tata turned to me and asked, *Why the long face?*

I told him there was nothing special. No sweets, no fruit, no bakery buns. Then he patted me on the back and Mama said she would make a cake, but I already knew that war cakes were nothing like regular cakes. And then Amina announced the package was not nearly enough for a family to live on for one month and Hana told her to not to be ungrateful and an argument started that made it seem kind of like a family celebration after all.

But I know what it's like to feel so disappointed that you want to — no, you have to — bite something really hard, like your own arm, someone else's arm, the edge of the kitchen table. And I never felt so disappointed as after that grade six contest. Not even after the Sarajevo electrical station, the one Tata said was one of the most modern in Europe, stopped powering the cinema and the lamp by my bed and the hot water tank. Or after forcing down one of Mama's stupid war cakes. Or after Arman blew up and they closed the elementary school for good.

Elle said that we were in demand, we were out from under, we were going to rule the school in grade seven, but without those plane tickets we were no closer to our dream than we'd been before.

Wasn't the whole point to win that trip to Orlando? Maybe some part of dumb ten-year-old me got it that timing can be everything. CristElle would never have quite the same magic. *Star Search* would go off the air. The war would end before we could tell the judges I was a poor little refugee with big dreams, show them our stuff and become superstars.

2

October 1, 1999
From: CristElle@hotmail.com
To: Spaho123@hotmail.com
Subject line: hope you're fricking happy

I was doing fine. Then I found that yellow T-shirt with the crystal ball logo Amina made us with her first paycheck from Robin's Donuts. I thought I lost it but it was in the front closet behind a box of New Year's hats Mindy said she was taking to the children's hospital.

I remember when I came up with CristElle you were eating Cheerios out of the box and I grabbed it and poured some on your head because I was so pumped. And your mama threw knives at me with her eyes but I didn't care because it was so brilliant and we were going to clean up the cereal anyway.

But here's the thing. That shirt is as big as a fricking tent and it's like that girl who did that, she's a different person, and it's like I'm jealous of her even though she had to wear a tent. So I hope you're happy now that I'm as screwed up as u.

October 3, 1999
From: CristElle@hotmail.com
To: Spaho123@hotmail.com
Subject line: beached whale

I fricking keep thinking of when we went to the wading pool near the community club. It was the summer before grade 7 and I wanted to go to the real one at Kildonan Park so bad but u couldn't do your laps to get out of the kiddie area.

It was just us and a bunch of moms with toddlers, and I grabbed a pail and poured icy pee water over your head and one of the moms took pity on u and gave u her kid's super soaker. Back then it didn't matter that I was still a fat piece of blubber and u were a foreign freak. U didn't care that we were running around in freezing toddler urine or that the kiddies and moms thought we were crazy or that your bathing suit was too baggy for your lily white butt, because u never cared. It's one of the things I loved about u. Like at the end of the summer when we went back just for fun and that whole daycare was hogging the pool. So we were lying on our towels looking up at the canker worms eating the trees clear of leaves when that guy said, WATCH OUT FOR THE BEACHED WHALE.

I swear it must have been heat stroke or something, but u got up and went over to them and said something like, what was that? And he said, what was what? And you said, you know what. Then one of the daycare workers came and asked if there was a problem and u said, this guy is being a douchebag.

U didn't even know what it meant! I had to drag u away and u told me Hana's friend always called her boss that. But not to his face, I said. And u just shrugged like that was beside the point. I couldn't believe it. I still can't believe it.

Then I was thinking how we watched *Titanic* sixteen times and I know this because for some stupid fricking reason I saved all the tickets. Maybe I'm going to end up like Mindy, drowning in my own garbage. I think I loved that movie so much because Rose isn't skinny, she's luscious and round and that's the only reason she lives. She's like her own life raft and poor bony Jack with his sad story and big dreams sinks like a rock.

And now whenever I dream about swimming, I'm always so happy and I'm always still fat.

But here's the thing. U loved *Titanic*, too, I know u did, but u never cried and that got me thinking, have I ever seen u cry? I don't think so and that is fricking WEIRD since you are such a giant baby mama's boy. How could I be so stupid?

How did I not notice that instead of some clueless knight in shining pasty white you were actually the WORST of the worst???

October 4, 1999
From: CristElle@hotmail.com
To: Spaho123@hotmail.com
Subject line: swan dive

When we were kids, we did not fit in. We were classic misfits. Jimmy says all good stories have misfit heroes. Where u went wrong was u took a swan dive from misfit to fricking outcast.

I'm going to cut up that T-shirt into little strips and give it to Amanda-P's hamster to use as toilet paper.

October 5, 1999

Budgie asked this morning if I'm ready to talk about more recent events, and I answered with my own question, which I know is the oldest trick in the book. *Like what?* She looked tired and I wondered if she might be getting sick again. She was wearing that bright green sweater and it made her pink skin look almost purple.

Like why you're here.

I didn't take the bait, so she had to keep fishing.

Why do you think you're here, Laz-Aaar?

I told Budgie I wasn't ready to talk about it. She said okay, what did I want to talk about then? I told her maybe we should go in order, like grade seven next, even though it was not exactly a banner year.

Elle wasn't there for the first six weeks of school because Jimmy kept her in BC to provide a hands-on education into what he called the land of the spirit bear and its mysterious ways. Amina was on a tear because another thirty-seven people were blown up in the Markale and NATO was finally flying over the mountains and bombing the Chetniks, who were saying the city's defenders sent mortars to kill their own people to get sympathy in the West. She even started standing in the donut shop parking lot during her break, handing out flyers and trying to get people to sign a petition until her pimply supervisor told her to cut it out. She told me if I didn't get away from that idiot tube, she was going to smash it with a hammer.

So I joined the math club for a bit. There were only four of us and two of the grade eights just wanted to go on about quantum theory, which made it sound like the flux capacitor in *Back to the Future* maybe wasn't so far-fetched and after a while it kind of felt like I was back in the projector booth with my Deda Ilić, who secretly still said his prayers at night even though his wife and daughter were members of the Party. I was just a kid watching him box films and so he could go on about the Holy Spirit in rocks and stars and turtles and how not seeing is believing, just like those guys who acted like math club wasn't about numbers at all.

Then when Elle finally got back all she wanted to do was tell stories about sleeping bags so wet you had to wring them out like a dishcloth, or ticks the size of peanut M&M's, or Jimmy's friend who chained himself to trees for a living. She didn't wash her hair for the entire month of November because after a few weeks it was supposed to stop looking greasy and start to shine, except maybe she gave up too soon. I actually had to remind her that I didn't try out for the jazz choir because I wanted to spend time on our own stuff and she acted like this was all news to her.

I think after a while she figured out I was kind of mad because she made a big deal of my birthday.

Back in Bosnia, December 24 was just a usual day because the holidays went by the old Julian calendar. Elle always said I got totally ripped off when I came here and suddenly had to share my birthday with a fricking god, and in grade seven, she and Mindy brought over a cake that was roughly in the shape of our logo and Elle sang her own rendition of Adina Howard's "Freak Like Me." She also brought a big bottle of Mountain Dew and made a toast like it was champagne even though it looked like pee. *Here's to Cris who is twelve today, but doesn't look a day over eleven. Don't be in a rush to get to puberty, my late-blooming friend. Trust me. Keep that soprano and stay young and hair-free as long as you can.* She told Amina and me that fat girls mature early, which I know now means puberty, but then I didn't really want to know. Mama made *japrak* like she's done for every birthday since I can remember, even that freezing December of the siege. She made no fuss over the girls' birthdays, but for mine she somehow found cabbage and meat even if it was just enough for me, and there was cake even if it was war cake, and small presents even if it was just a pen flashlight and second-hand comic book that cost the earth, and there were guests even if it was just the neighbors coming to warm up at our fire in the stove lit for the party.

This time Elle got Mindy to make a thirty-dollar donation to Greenpeace in my name and Amina paid one of Mama's Filipino ladies to make us black rayon shirts with embroidered silver CristElle logos. Dajdža Drago and Sharon were in Florida but they chipped in with the rest of the family and bought me a Sega console as a combined Christmas/birthday present.

It was a pretty good night, except with the usual sniping after Elle left. Hana asked Mama if Elle looked thinner and Mama sniffed and said at least fatty's hair was washed. I think maybe she'd toasted too much with real wine.

Budgie said it sounded like a nice birthday, surrounded by friends and family, and I told her maybe, but then things went down the toilet. First the Dayton Peace Accords were signed in Paris, the Chetniks slunk down from the mountains and the siege was over. This meant Sarajevo was suddenly back in the news and Amina became the go-to refugee for the *Winnipeg Free Press*.

Just after the new year, the CBC brought cameras to the apartment because they wanted to talk to a regular Bosnian family after some militants fired a rocket-propelled grenade at a tram running down the main street of Sarajevo, killing a woman the same age as Mama. Elle and I worked on what my comments should be and we were pumped that I was going to be on TV but the reporters cut out the part where I said those militants obviously hadn't got the memo about peace.

Then a week later Nana Spaho had a stroke in her Sarajevo apartment and Amina went to Dajdža Drago behind Mama and Tata's back and Dajdža Drago gave Amina money to fly home to be with Tata's mama.

And then it was like our Winnipeg apartment was at war. Amina called home to say that Nana Spaho was a stubborn old bat who exaggerated her symptoms so she didn't have to leave her hellhole of a flat and come to Canada, and Mama told Amina that after all they'd done to keep her safe, if she carried on to Belgrade to see Baba and Deda Ilić while Serbia was still rattling sabers with the Albanians in Kosovo she would never speak to her again.

Budgie asked how I felt about all this and I said all I cared about was keeping CristElle on track. Before Elle left for Jimmy's in April we started focusing on "Another Night" by Real McCoy, but then our new principal, Mrs. Yaskiw, decided she didn't believe in facing one student off against another. Instead of a talent contest, she turned it into a talent *show*, and in the end I sang and Elle did her signature moves, but the whole thing didn't come close to before. Maybe without winners and losers, without all the drama and judgment and questions of justice served or justice denied, the whole thing seemed kind of pointless.

Soulgroan didn't even bother showing up.

October 6, 1999

I keep thinking about something Budgie said.

You have a good memory, Laz-Aaar. You can remember many things almost word for word. But not others. I want you to think about why that might be. Okay?

Amina loves to talk about this post-traumatic stuff and maybe Budgie thinks all my problems come from not remembering bad things that happened. But I do remember.

Amina told a reporter once that she remembered us huddling together around the dying fire while the shells fell and Mama's crystal glasses clanked and pinged like fairy music in the cupboards. And I was like, huh? Because she made it sound like poetry, and Elle says I don't have an ear for that and I should stick with math problems and other people's lyrics. So I might not remember that, but I do remember.

Like maybe four months after the start of the siege, I remember it was a perfect summer day, no clouds at all, when Baba and Deda Ilić closed the cinema for good. They brought all the leftover treats and the American-style popcorn machine across town to our apartment and Deda Ilić and Tata couldn't fit the machine up the stairs, so for the next six months while it lasted, we made popcorn every time someone in our building had a birthday. The oil and butter and the good ol' *pop-pop-popping* made it impossible not to smile at each other.

I remember the way Baba and Deda Ilić cried like the world was ending because Tata and Mama refused to go with them to the Dark Side in Belgrade, and I remember Mama letting me eat two Kakao Krem a day for weeks on end. I remember the exact last words my deda said to me when he left: *Your father wants to stay and defend his beloved city. But what does a schoolteacher know about such things?* And I remember hating him for leaving more than I ever thought it was possible to hate anyone.

Even then I knew he was just an old man who'd spent most of his life acting like owning a cinema was like owning a professional sports team or something. But when push came to shove he left our cinema to the pigeons and the snipers and he was no better than some Belgrade-armed Chetnik hidden in a broken window.

Now I've done something way worse than he ever did, and Elle hates me more than I ever hated anyone, even my own deda.

October 7, 1999

Mama told me I had to go to the tailor shop tomorrow and learn how to work the cash register and I could hear Elle's voice, like she was talking in my head.

You are dead to me. You are more than dead to me. It's like you never came here. You were never born. You never existed.

Then Sara dropped me off at Budgie's office and drove away while I was still slamming the door and my heart was beating really fast and I wanted to chase after her car, maybe grab onto a side mirror like in the movies and let her drag me all the way home.

When I sat down I thought my heart might jump out of my mouth and Budgie was wearing a shiny yellow blouse that pulled at the buttons, very puffed out at the chest and budgie-like, and she cocked her head to the side and asked if I was okay and I said I can't talk about what happened yet.

She said, *Laz-Aaar, this is your story, you tell it your way. I'm not going anywhere.* And I said we needed to keep going, from the beginning of CristElle and all the way through to Ivan, and the end.

I told her that the first week of grade eight, Elle came back from Jimmy's a vegan. She had to explain to me what that was and then I had to explain to Mama that some people not only didn't eat dead animals, but they didn't eat any animal by-products.

Elle said, *Human beings are the only animals who drink milk from other animals* and Amina said, *We're also the only animals that watch TV or drive armored vehicles*, and Elle said she didn't get the point. Amina said, *You're not comparing apples to apples* and Elle said, *Who said anything about apples?*

And Amina laughed, because when it came to Elle she let a lot of things go that she normally wouldn't.

Mama, though, wouldn't stop going on. *I neber heard of such a thing. The ones who come up with these crazy ideas neber been hungry. It's easy to be big hero when you got around more than you could eat in a year.*

I told her this was the new thing, because the mass cultivation of cows for milk and beef was destroying the earth and Jimmy predicted that New Orleans would be under water and we'd all be vegans by 2020. Mama said this Jimmy was an idiot and even Tata said some people have never even met someone who butchers his own meat so don't understand how superior such livestock tastes.

Budgie sucked on her pen and smiled. *Like me*, she said, and I told her Tata's father was a halal butcher so it was easy for him to say.

But it was around this time that Elle started shrinking a bit, like a snow bank during a spring thaw. I didn't even notice until Hana told Mama that it was impossible for Elle to stay so *debeo* eating nothing but *kunić* food. I didn't tell them that Elle still ate lots of things that rabbits don't eat, like corn chips and Frosted Flakes and Slurpees. It was just maybe hard to stay quite so fat when you're not eating handfuls of grated mozzarella or drinking cartons of chocolate milk.

Budgie asked if I thought Elle had a problem with food, and I said her only problem was she liked it too much. Then she wanted to know if I thought Elle's weight bothered her and I told her I didn't know, I'm not a mind reader, but a couple of months after we met, Mindy said maybe Elle should go to a counselor about getting healthier and Elle accused her of giving in to the fashion police and hating her own daughter's body because it didn't fit the manufactured mold of beauty.

Elle said a lot of stuff, though. Like she told me organized activities were not for a free-wheeling spirit like hers but then she decided we should try out for the Divisional Middle School Jazz Choir. I said, *I thought you said you weren't a joiner*, and she acted like I was out of line for even bringing it up. *What the what, Cris? How long ago was that? People change, you know. What are you worried about anyway? You'll make it in no problem. Last year Dubé acted like you were her personal little protegé.*

Budgie wanted to know if I thought Elle felt bad because I had such a good voice and I said I don't know, I'm not a mind reader, which was kind of an a-hole thing to keep saying, but I was suddenly so tired of talking, talking, talking, even though I just told her I needed to tell her this.

What I should have said was I didn't need Elle to tell me that people change. Families change, cities change, people come and go, whole countries come and go. And this was no different, because nothing was the same after we made the choir.

I told Budgie that in the end, Elle and I auditioned at the same time in the basement of Westwood United, where it smelled like a mix of craft glue and toilet cleaner, and Elle told Ms. Gulliano we'd been an inseparable singing team since we were ten. That's also when we met Amanda-P, who Elle said was panda bear cute. There were three Amandas from three different schools who ended up in jazz choir and she was the only one whose family was from the Philippines and who actually talked to us when she didn't have to.

Budgie said, *So you two made a friend*, and I told her Elle said the thing with girls like Amanda-P is they make it their mission in life to be nice to every person they meet not because they like you but because it's their mission. Like even though the year had just started and we all barely knew each other, she invited every single person in the choir to her little sister's birthday party. And the thing is, I was so sure that when Elle opened the fancy pink invitation she would have a snark attack and say no way. But instead she said this was our chance to meet people and what else did we have to do besides sit around and watch *Dumb and Dumber* again. I told her I'd made some money helping Tata unload paint cans at the recycling depot and I was going to buy Bust-A-Move 2 for the Sega and she said we could do that anytime.

Mama acted like this was the first party I'd ever been invited to, which I guess it was, at least in Winnipeg, and Hana and Sara had a good time talking about what to buy for a Filipino kid none of us had ever met.

In the end Sara went to the grocery store and had them wrap up some pink roses in fancy paper and there were over a hundred people at the Filipino cultural center, mostly crowding by the buffet and karaoke machine. Amanda-P's seven-year-old sister was wearing a mini ballgown that looked like it was made of purple tinfoil. She took the flowers from me with a little curtsy and kind of glared at Elle.

Budgie said people from Old World cultures tend to know a thing or two about etiquette, and I said all I know is that Elle acted like she didn't want to be there even though she's the one who wanted to go. Amanda-P introduced us to her cousin Marc who had pimples all over his forehead and was holding hands with Alyssa from the choir. Elle pulled me aside and said that Alyssa was even paler than me, not bad if you liked the undead type. She complained about the lack of vegan options and the three ridiculous dresses the kid changed in and out of like some pop star and the tipsy old people hogging the karaoke. She went on and on about how kids our age who thought they were part of a real couple were just little children playing at the game of love.

It's so ridiculous. Some of them have been at it since grade six, like they have any clue about real sexual attraction yet. I told her I heard Filipinos traditionally make a really big deal of certain birthdays, just like the Jews, and she laughed like she couldn't believe how dumb I was. *We're not even talking about that anymore.*

Budgie wanted to know how I felt about kids that age dating, and I said it was kind of like the kids at school who smoked behind the garbage bin. The smokers I knew — my deda, my tata, soldiers from every side — they fixed boilers and cleaned guns with a cigarette hanging off their lip like they were born with it. They puffed like it was as natural to them as breathing air. The boys behind the bin sharing a pack stolen from their grandma's purse had no idea.

Elle said we didn't have to pretend, except then she started talking about her own birthday party. I said, *Since when you do care about that stuff,* and she said, *You have birthday parties,* and I said, *Not really, it's just you and Mindy and my family and it's Christmas.* Besides, my thirteenth had not exactly been a great time since Mama had the flu and Elle said Mindy had the blues and we mostly sat around playing Olympic Summer Games: Atlanta 1996.

Elle usually spent April at Jimmy's but he was in Thailand that year so she used Mindy's credit card to book Angelino's because they allowed minors in the lounge for family karaoke on Sunday afternoons. I said CristElle should prepare something because it had been a while and the sleeves on my shirt were getting so short I couldn't wear it much longer but Elle kept stalling and finding excuses not to rehearse.

On the day of the party I went early with Mindy and it was like Elle was competing in the talent contest all over again. She kept pacing around the empty lounge until Amanda-P and Alyssa and Marc came. Budgie asked me why I thought Elle was so nervous and I said I didn't know since I was the only one doing a prepared performance.

I'd decided to go back to some classic songwriting with Elton's "Candle in the Wind," which was huge that year, and when I was finished Elle came and threw her arms around me and told me the song was lame pop nostalgia but I was da bomb and she kissed my ear. Then Amanda-P asked how long we'd been going out, and Elle said, *Oh god, we've known each other forever.*

Budgie sucked her pen. *Things were changing.*

Elle would have said, *No shit, birdbrain.*

October 8, 1999

The deal is, if I don't go to school I have to go to the tailor shop. The place is full of nothing but ladies, which is the story of my life. Mama gets testy with customers who want their pants hemmed while they wait. She says, *What you think these ladies are machines?* Maybe she has no sense of customer service because she was a Party member and worked in an office before. Maybe they want me to help out with the cash because Mama's bad for business.

Amina says now that the trams are running in Sarajevo and life is returning to some kind of normal, those who took up arms against their neighbors are living in their own personal hell.

Maybe working in the tailor shop is part of my punishment for what I did to Elle.

October 11, 1999

Ivan came in grade nine, the first one in choir to have gelled hair and invisible braces.

But what if he didn't? What if his dad never got the job as first French horn with the symphony? What if he never moved here from Montreal? Would things have unraveled anyway? Like if Slobodan Milošević had never been born, or if he'd never taken an interest in crazy Serbian nationalist politics, would the war still have happened?

Can one single person change the course of history? Or are the quantum guys right and none of it matters because it's all happening anyway?

October 12, 1999

It snowed a bit this morning, the kind that pretty much melts right away, and Sara almost got into an accident on the way to the session. Unlike Tata, she looks at me all the time and says things like, *You're old enough to take the bus, you know. They're not doing you any favors by babying you.*

Budgie looked tired again, but maybe it was just the hair. She got it cut short with one side longer than the other and dyed oranger than before. It was like her haircut was younger than her face, and the whole thing made her even more like a bird, with its head cocked sideways and bright feathers ruffled. It kind of freaked me out because it's like maybe she's somehow reading this when I'm not around and testing to see how crazy I can get.

There's something wrong with my psychiatrist. She is not a mammal.

She wanted to know when young people start dating in Bosnia and I said I didn't know, probably the same as here. As far back as I can remember Hana was always bringing home boys who Tata said were all the same. *They stand in the kitchen doorway in their tight jeans, every single one of them, rocking back and forth on the balls of their feet, smelling like soap.*

Amina was sixteen when the siege started and one day she brought home a Jew named Ira who had a giant head of curly hair and he gave me a Kakao Krem, which was nice except we had about six hundred of them stockpiled from when Deda closed down the cinema. Amina cried and cried when he left a few months later and Tata pulled her on his lap like she was still small and said, *The Jews have somewhere to go, so they are going, malo kokoška. After this insanity is over they'll be back. This city is their ciy too.*

I hadn't thought of that in a long time, how Tata used to call Amina his little hen.

Budgie asked if we should talk about how things were changing and I told her everything changed when we became freshmen. That's what they say in American movies, but I guess for us it was just grade nine. Elle said it sucked because we were just stupid little music geeks and suddenly there's some code we were supposed to understand just because we were in high school. She said I was lucky because I was blissfully oblivious to social cues.

All I knew is that suddenly CristElle was just some funny kids' thing we used to do and a choir festival in Fargo, North Dakota, was the trip of a lifetime.

Budgie said let's talk about Fargo then. Like it was that simple, because when Elle came back from Jimmy's after the Labor Day weekend, she was a lot skinnier. But that wasn't the only change. She said it was time to cut, slash and burn her lifelong nemesis, fat.

Turns out Frieda was into selling herbal detox plants and hiking and when I asked Elle what was the difference between hiking and walking, she said hiking was in the mountains. I said in Bosnia we had lots of mountains and we walked in them all the time and she told me I was just being an a-hole because hiking was in *nature*.

That year Elle went on and on about how you couldn't even walk in this Arctic outpost of a city and she sounded like Hana who could never get used to the dry cold. She kept saying she was going to move to Texas and Amina would tell her to go ahead, go get shot in a McDonald's in gun-slinging America, and Sara would say they could both go to hell as long she didn't have to listen to them.

Budgie said maybe there were too many people in that little apartment, which was only partly true. By grade nine Hana was barely there anymore because she was always at her sugar daddy's, or at least that's what Elle called him. Riel is actually only six years older than Hana and he's her husband now and he isn't exactly rich. He just has a steady job with Manitoba Public Insurance and drives a two-seater Mazda that's nicer than anything Dajdža Drago ever had. Sara was usually working at the mall or going to college part-time to get some diploma for running a business, or staying at a friend's.

So it was mostly just Amina driving Mama and Tata crazy by saying that now that the siege had ended and the Serbs had turned their attention to their old territories in Kosovo and NATO was finally taking things seriously, she was going back to Sarajevo. She said she must bear witness to what happened to our nice flat, to our beloved cinema, to our poor old Nana Spaho. She wanted to defend what was rightfully still ours from the hucksters and opportunists out to profit from the spoils of war. She wanted to help rebuild her bruised, battered and embittered homeland.

Mama told her that it was bad enough having her parents in Belgrade where the war-mongers in Kosovo were still in a fever that wouldn't break. And if Amina didn't stop talking about returning to that mess she would not only hide her passport but disown her as a daughter.

Amina and Mama, at least, didn't change.

——

After Elle started getting skinny and before Ivan came, maybe that was CristElle's swan song.

Most weekends I would pick songs and do vocals and Elle would throw herself around the living room trying to work up a sweat. She only wanted to do stuff with a good aerobic beat and we did some straight-ahead forgettable pop like Backstreet Boys and Puff Daddy. Amina said we were still CristElle, only in its purest, most personal, most joyful form. We still laughed our heads off at the way Mindy's poodle hair looked right after she woke up and the way Mama picked her nose when she thought no one was looking. We still rented movies and Elle still threw popcorn in the air and never managed to catch it in her mouth, only it was unbuttered instead of buttered.

For Christmas Amina helped me buy Elle Susan Powter's video, *Burn Fat and Get Fit!* and Elle got me Bass Fishing for the Sega with Mindy's credit card. She said Tata and I could pretend we were fishing by some remote mountain stream that no one could pronounce. On New Year's Day, Tata said, *This crazy game, it's got me hooked*, and Mama said he should speak in English but she was laughing.

At home when it was just the two of us Elle was her usual self, but around school it was different. She kept telling me what people were saying about her. Like Amanda-P had abandoned us for a lonely Brazilian exchange student named Hugo but thought Elle looked a bit like Alicia Silverstone. Or Ingrid Bloke, who thought she had the best soprano in the choir, had never noticed Elle had a heart-shaped face before. Or Izzie Troia, who did have the best soprano, wanted to go shopping with Elle when she bought her whole new size 6 wardrobe.

And when she talked to any of them, it's like she had one line that she rehearsed and repeated. *I'm just sticking to the plan. Less fat in, less fat round.*

Budgie asked how I thought the girls made Elle feel and I said all I knew was that in the spring Elle took off to Jimmy's and stayed there all of March and all of April and Ms. Gulliano nearly kicked her out of choir because how are you supposed to learn group pieces for an international engagement when you're not there?

Budgie wanted to know if it was hard for me while Elle was gone and I told her Mama got it in her head that I needed to get out of the house because it was getting lighter outside, spring was coming no matter how much snow was left, and I was sitting playing Bug! on the Sega like an invalid.

Even Tata said, *You're still young, what are you doing in here with us old people?* Once Amina joined in I didn't stand a chance because she'd actually gone to the school and brought me sign-up forms for afterschool games club, intramural volleyball and guitar.

Budgie said, *Your family cares about you very much,* and I told her caring about someone and knowing what's best for them are not the same thing. Just because I could play Sega Worldwide Soccer forever didn't mean I was cut out for sports. At least guitar was music, but I think my skin must be unusually soft because after the first two sessions the ends of my fingers were nothing but blisters. That left gaming club, or Role Play Rollers, which Ivan said if anyone ever called it that he was never coming back.

Budgie asked who Ivan was and I realized she really didn't know. Mama and Tata wouldn't have told her anything because they'd only seen him once for maybe five minutes and he was wearing a Halloween costume.

It's weird to think that my own parents could pass Ivan on the street and have no idea who he was or what he must think of me now.

I told Budgie that when I met Ivan he'd only been at our school for a few weeks but was already running his own game. I walked into gaming club and he told me to sit down and he would work me into the adventure as a dwarf who'd been laid up with sleeping sickness and was just re-joining his party. I remember thinking he talked kind of the same as Amina, like everything that came out of his mouth was important — weapons and powers and mon-sters, except Ivan's were all made up.

That was the best day I had in a while because role play-ing was kind of like Sega's Dragon Force except you played with other people so Mama and Tata and Amina could shut up and stop worrying about me.

Budgie said, *So you made a new friend.*

I told her every choir geek was friends with Ivan.

I was the one who met Ivan first, before Elle even saw him in choir and said he reminded her of Johnny Depp. She didn't even notice him that first day after she got back from Jimmy's. She was rushing out of the choir room and I yelled to ask her if she was coming over and she said she needed to walk first and I asked if Mindy's car was dead again and she said no she needed to walk and I asked where and she looked ready to hit me.

Nowhere. Just walk.

That's when Ivan appeared out of nowhere, like he had the power of invisibility.

Who's that?

Elle, I said. *She's been at her dad's.*

You two an item?

I wasn't sure what this meant, so I took a guess. *We've known each other forever.*

And he nodded slowly, like he was filing it away for future reference.

I've been thinking about stars. We talked about them in science last year and Ivan knew everything about black dwarfs and red dwarfs and supernovas. But I was just thinking how stars are held together by their own gravity until things heat up too much, and then they collapse on themselves, and then boom.

It's like me and Mama and Tata and Sara and Amina and Hana were tight as a burning star until the siege. Then we closed in and collided, and the apartment in Winnipeg was the shockwave that sent us flying into space.

Now we're just rocky planets who might as well not be in the same galaxy.

I know what Elle would say. She'd say stars give her the creeps because they make her feel like a pointless little ant who lives and dies in the blink of an eye.

October 13, 1999

Before we finished the session, Budgie asked about Fargo again and I told her there was nothing really to say because it was just a school trip. Spend four and a half hours on a bus, sing at the civic auditorium that looked like a concrete bunker, go back to the hotel, swim in the pool, go to bed, wake up, eat cold waffles from the breakfast buffet, spend four and a half hours on the bus again.

But I've been thinking about that night in Fargo, how anyone with eyes could see that Elle was different. When she sat on Ivan's shoulders in the pool, trying to knock Ingrid off Scottie Abrams and Izzie off Luke Chipeway, she looked just like any other girl. With their wet hair it was hard to tell who was who.

But she was acting like any other girl too. They kept yelling at me to come in, or saying they were going to throw me in, but I was pretty sure they didn't really care if I was with them or not. It's like they were a bunch of dolphins jumping around in the water playing some game I didn't understand. And it's like Elle was splashing ten feet away from me but I was a rocky planet all by myself.

I'm doing this at the tailor shop because there's nothing to do but listen to the drill of the sewing needles or watch the Filipino soaps they play on the VCR.

I keep thinking about Hana's wedding. I'm pretty sure once a dead star explodes, that's it. There's no going back together, not even for a special occasion, but Ivan said the supernova explosion can sometimes briefly outshine its entire home galaxy.

I remember Elle said she didn't believe in the paternalistic institution of marriage and that Frieda said it was an outdated custom invented for legal and financial reasons and was exclusionary toward gays and singles. I asked her why she wanted to come to Hana's then and she said she'd never been to a wedding so it was an experience.

For the reception Amina wanted me to sing "Can't Help Falling in Love," except the Elvis Presley version. But it didn't feel right, maybe because it felt like CristElle's song and because lightning pretty much never strikes twice.

I looked into "As Long as You Love Me" by the Backstreet Boys, but Elle said it was the processed cheese of love songs and I could never listen to it again without thinking about that. She played Depeche Mode's "Somebody" for Hana, who actually liked it because she remembered the band from the clubs back in Sarajevo. I asked them if they were serious because those guys looked like zombies with their powder white faces and light-socket hair, and Elle said they were what Ivan called mid-80s New Wave retro. She said Ivan had a CD music collection that took up two walls of his bedroom.

But I still thought that song was just as lame as the Backstreet Boys. We'd done The Beatles "I Will" as part of our pop repertoire in jazz choir and I prepared that for a few weeks until Hana finally said Riel was a big fan of Bryan Adams, the Canadian with the blotchy skin, and I ended up with his okay hit, "Everything I Do, I Do It for You."

Riel was from a French Catholic family so Hana had to take marriage preparation classes for three months and learn about the Pope and stuff, which actually seemed to fire up Tata for a while. He grumbled in Bosnian whenever the wedding mass or the priest came up.

This is what Yugoslavia worked so hard to end. All the pomp and superstitions and to-do. You couldn't have dragged me into that Orthodox gold-leaf monstrosity to marry your mother and I never would have asked her to pledge her love to me in my mother's mosque.

In the end it was so sticky hot in the church and there was so much sitting down and getting up that Amina fainted and Sara said she was just mad about not being in the wedding party and trying to steal Hana's show. I thought Elle would find the whole thing completely hilarious, but instead she looked like she was going to cry.

Mindy had bought her a yellow dress from the mall and her silver sandals had skinny heels that made her walk funny. When I asked her what was up, she said she just couldn't stand it when everyone was trying so hard and everything still went to shit, and I almost said this is nothing when it comes to trying hard and things still being shit.

Instead I told her that the party was the real thing and it would be tight, and she said, *Ivan always says tight*, and I said, *Everyone says tight*, and she said, *Only because Ivan says it.*

At the reception the room was smaller than I thought it would be and a hundred people looked like fewer than I imagined. Dajdža Drago and Sharon had bought all the flowers, these towering red birds of paradise that looked like they were trying to eat you, and it was hard to see the person across the table. Mama said they were very sophisticated and modern and Tata spent a lot of time outside smoking. Elle kept asking me who people were and I had to keep saying I had no idea because the whole place was pretty much the groom's side.

After dinner, though, Tata actually made a toast in English, and he told everyone how much it meant to him to

95

have his first child settled in Canada with a fine young man and dreams for the future and everyone cried except for me and Amina, who kept her face blank and her eyes in her lap, probably thinking about the terrible things the Serbs were doing to Muslims in Kosovo right then. After Hana and Riel danced to Shania Twain's "From This Moment On," the DJ played "Can't Help Falling in Love," the Elvis Presley version, and Amina kept poking Elle and me until we got up.

And the funny thing is, I couldn't even count the times Elle and I danced together in our lives, danced like we didn't give two shits what anybody thought, but it was never like this, so close that we could feel each other breathing. It's different when you're not just touching someone but holding them, and your fingers are resting on that super soft place right under their hairline.

It wasn't like hugging Mama and the girls with their thick hair and square shoulders. Elle's hair was pulled up in a braid that Sara did for her and that just left the baby hairs at the bottom of her neck. I don't know if I ever felt anything so soft, even on a kitten, and I started thinking about Elle's eyes for the first time, because that afternoon, coming out of the steamy church into the burning sun, I noticed they were not brown, not green, but hazel — like one of Winnipeg's mud-bottom rivers on a clear day. It's like I was suddenly noticing stupid little things like the sound of her high heels clicking on the dance floor or the bump of her knee against the inside of my leg or the cinnamon smell of her breathing because she'd splurged and eaten the whole apple tart for dessert.

Then the song was over and we were back at the table and Sara was saying, *Nice shambling, Cris.* And what's funny is I barely remember singing that stupid Bryan Adams song I'd worked so hard on. A bunch of Riel's relatives came up afterwards and said nice stuff but mostly I just remember Elle. I remember coming back from the mic at the front and her sitting with the edge of the white tablecloth bunched in her fist, very unladylike, and saying, *That song is so whatever. But I'm still crying. What the hell?* And I remember not knowing what to say and having to go outside where Tata was smoking and him saying in English, *This things, they are so bremenit, church or mosque or no. This times a man just needs some air, son.*

He didn't know the English for *bremenit*, and when I looked it up later, the closest word was *fraught*.

October 14, 1999

Mama just told me Budgie called and her mom died last night and she's going to Toronto, which means no sessions for maybe a week. I didn't know her mom was even sick.

I guess I don't know much about Budgie except she has a little hatchling that carries germs home from the daycare. Maybe talking about her daughter is Budgie's way of promoting birth control to a teenager only there isn't much chance of me *gettin' busy*, as Elle would say, any time soon. There's no chance of anything, really, so maybe I might as well be a ghost.

In all the movies ghosts come back because they have some kind of unfinished business, but what about during a war? I mean, shouldn't there be nothing but ghosts wandering around after a war?

I was thinking about how I know almost nothing about Budgie and she knows so much about me because she is the professional and I am the patient, but this kind of thing happens in real life all the time. Like I know way more about Amina, who pretty much says whatever she thinks, than Sara, who sits painting her nails and I have no idea if she's thinking about Nana Spaho's syrupy *tulumba* or some serial killer she's started writing to in prison.

For a long time I thought I knew Elle pretty much as well as I knew myself but turns out I barely knew either one of us.

Ivan told us that his uncle, who lives in California and used to write for a sitcom called *Who's the Boss*, told him a definition for comedy. Tragedy is when I stub my toe. Comedy is when you fall in an open manhole and die.

I didn't get it until just now, on my bed in my underwear, feeling kind of relieved that I'm off the hook for a few days because someone's mom died.

When we left Sarajevo through the tunnel, I wasn't really scared because we were all together and I was too happy to be doing something other than sitting around pretending I wasn't jealous of Arman, who maybe only had one leg left but at least escaped the four walls of his apartment.

The only thing that freaked me out was the moths around the overhead lights. I mean, how did they get down there?

I've been thinking that Ivan's like a light bulb dangling from a ceiling at night and all the rest of us are bugs. Mama said once that Elle tried way too hard to be *drugačiji* all the time and Amina said she made it sound like being different was a lifestyle choice, but even Elle was like the rest of us with Ivan. Which when I think about Elle and Ivan, is kind of rich — as in Elle saying, *Ms. Boehm thinks I might have anorexia? Now that is rich coming from pancake butt* — because I was really friends with Ivan first.

Probably the only reason I kept going to gaming club was because I had to know what Ivan the Dungeon Master would come up with next. Some people said he had to be a genius to create his own game and keep track of the rules without even a manual, but Elle claimed it was all about his *tripping tight imagination*. Which was rich, considering she'd never even played with us and whenever I tried to explain it to her she'd be *yadda-yadda-yadda, whatever*, because coming from me it sounded like a total a waste of time.

Which it kind of was, because at least with CristElle we were working toward something. We had a goal, we had real dreams. After a couple months into the game I said to Ivan that in the real world you could be the smartest and the strongest, with a cloak of invisibility, even, and still get taken out by some a-hole with bad aim and a Russian howitzer. He just laughed and told me, *Don't overthink it, dude*, and I laughed too, even though I still think I had a point.

Since it's almost Halloween, every commercial on TV right now is trying to be spooky, even ones for dish detergent and minivans. No matter what Mama says about Belgrade and Sarajevo being nothing but terrible phantoms of their former selves, part of me wishes I could go visit my grandparents in the crazy Balkans because at least they don't do the whole Halloween thing.

I'm not sure who came up with such a stupid holiday but even when we were back in grade six and Elle couldn't wait to show me all the plastic skeletons and fake blood that Mindy picked up at Liquidation World, I didn't get it. I didn't get the big thrill of pretending to be scared or pretending to be someone else and Elle said that's because I'm too literal for my own good. *Since when are you afraid to let your freak flag fly?* she said. I asked what she meant and she just groaned and said I was not a creative person.

I keep thinking of the Halloween party in Amanda-P's church basement, which was only a year ago but feels like ages, like way back when the Serbs were still poor victims of the Croatian Nazi Ustasha or the relentless Ottoman Empire, instead of the bad guys out for revenge.

When the invitations came out I told Elle I didn't feel like hanging out with Amanda-P's super-friendly Catholic Church Alliance friends, and Elle called me a *fricking jam tart*. But I stayed home anyway, even though there were no games coming out for the Sega anymore and there was no way I was getting my hands on a Nintendo until birthday/ Christmas. Mama asked why I wasn't going *to do the trick or treating* and I told her that was only for kids and then she came over and rubbed my cheek with her onion-smelling fingers and said I shouldn't be in any hurry to grow up and I pushed her hand away and she turned to Tata and said, *You see that moodiness I'm telling you about.* And he just sighed and said, *You should be out with friends your age, enjoying yourself.*

Then there was a knock at the door and Amina let in Elle and Ivan.

I didn't know who they were supposed to be at first — Elle in a short red wig and black suit and Ivan with a sketchy beard and sunglasses in the same suit — so Elle started singing "I Saved the World Today," which I was supposed to recognize. She gave me her *duh?* look, then said, the *Eurythmics?* Like I was supposed to know some duo from the early eighties who hadn't played together in years.

But that was the thing with Ivan. His dad wasn't just a symphony musician, he also collected jazz records and had been in a hard rock band called Juice Me. Ivan knew about songs from way before we were born and about songs that hadn't even come out yet.

He made a peace sign and Elle gave me her *duh?* look again and explained their new album was called *Peace*. Ivan told Amina that they'd gone with Annie and Dave's current incarnation because Elle suited red better than platinum and there was no way he was going with Dave's blond perm. Amina said they looked great but she was getting tired of pop stars who go on and on about how concerned they are about global conflict while sitting in their obscene mansions in their hypocritical countries.

Ivan and Elle ignored her and told me to get on a costume because they weren't going without me. I said I didn't have anything to wear and Elle went around the apartment looking through closets and drawers with Mama until they wrapped me in Tata's bathrobe and drew a shaggy beard on my face. Ivan made a sign that said *The End Is Near! Jesus Saves!* and when Tata asked what I was supposed to be, Elle said, *A crazy street person* and I said, *We're going to a church,* and Tata laughed until he choked on his bread and had to go have something to drink.

Then we were in the church basement that was decorated like a haunted house and there were homemade brownies with about three times too many walnuts and games like everyone trying to pass an orange around a circle only using their necks. I passed it to Elle no problem because we were the same height and neither one of us is ticklish and we know how each other move, but Elle took maybe twelve tries passing it to Ivan and they had the whole place cheering for them because Izzie told me later she heard they'd smuggled a few beer in Ivan's guitar case.

Then Ivan and Elle, who insisted we call them Annie and Dave, sat talking together most of the night. He was in charge of the CD player and kept playing a Cincinnati band he'd discovered called Ass Ponys, whose singer couldn't sing and the lyrics were just stupid. Everyone kept asking for more and when I asked how they could listen to that shit, Elle asked if I'd ever heard of irony.

I was eight when I overheard Tata tell a joke. *What's the difference between Sarajevo and Auschwitz? Auschwitz at least had a regular gas supply.* When I asked him what Auschwitz was, he didn't tell me it was a concentration camp where Jews were sent to the gas chambers. He just said, *Never mind. Just remember, irony is for amateurs. It's the black humor that cuts deep.*

I had no clue what he was talking about, of course, because I was eight. But years later in that church basement, I knew Elle had crossed the line and officially defected from CristElle forever.

Afterwards Amina asked me if I knew Annie Lennox and Dave Stewart used to be married and I said no, and she said Ivan had the untrustworthy air of a lot of Russians and I told her I didn't think he was actually Russian, his parents probably just liked the name. She said that was so typical, whatever that meant, and also did I know that the reunited Eurythmics had the nerve to launch their *Peace* album on a Greenpeace ship, as if that made them some kind of heroes.

Maybe Elle was right about me being too literal about Halloween. Maybe you can just overdose on pretending. Like let's pretend we're all one happy Yugoslav people. Let's pretend we're all ancient enemies who would rather blow each other up than share a sidewalk. Let's pretend everything is okay and light the candles on a tasteless cake.

But what I want to know is how does that fit with all the lies that came later?

Is pretending the same as lying?

October 16, 1999

It was almost the end of November when Mama made me
go to the doctor. I remember because there still wasn't any
snow, which almost never happens, and Ivan and I were
walking around with Elle every day after school. The flat
Winnipeg lawns were brown and the giant elm trees were
gray and their favorite topic was the choir trip to Toronto
which wasn't going to happen for another six months.

Ivan went on about other things, too, like how when
the Advanced edition of the Dungeons & Dragons Mon-
ster Manual came out, it showed the harpies and succubi
with naked breasts so some Christian group tried to shut
the whole thing down. Or how recent studies show that
group singing can be therapeutic even when the sound pro-
duced is of mediocre quality. Or how his dad met the
original drummer from Black Sabbath before they fired
him for being a drunk.

I told them the Yugoslav group Riva came to my grandparents' cinema once and Ivan asked if he'd know any of
their stuff. I told him "Rock Me" won the 1989 Eurovision
Song Contest and Elle said, *What the hell is a Eurovision Song
Contest?* and I tried to explain but they'd already moved on
to something else.

This whole time, though, when we were walking around
the ugly November streets and Elle had little purple weights
velcroed onto her ankles for an extra workout and Ivan
talked and talked so we couldn't listen to music, Mama
kept worrying that there was something wrong with me.
She said I was too skinny and pale, and that I should find
some sport to take up or some girl to court, like young boys
the world over. Mama always said that I was going to be a

late bloomer, which turns out was maybe just a polite way of saying I was behind. Because once Elle was skinnier and blow-dried her hair every morning and wore washed-out jeans from the mall, it was like Mama suddenly thought she was good enough for her son. It didn't matter that I was the youngest in my class or looked young for my age. Elle was a pretty girl who put up with me so what was I waiting for?

I told the doctor I was walking a lot and not drinking as many Slurpees and junk so I'd probably lost a few pounds. He told Mama that I was built slim and it wasn't abnormal for boys to not see hair or penis growth or have their voices change until fifteen. Mama said, *He's fifteen in a few weeks*, and the doctor said, *As I said ...*

All I knew was that every morning I woke up with my *kurac* hard as a Eurovision microphone except I couldn't tell Mama that.

So I was thinking that last Halloween, that was the end of the end of CristElle.

But that doctor's appointment. That was the beginning of the end of me.

3

October 15, 1999
From: CristElle@hotmail.com
To: Spaho123@hotmail.com
Subject line: oh my fricking god your hair

I found a pic of us from Hana's wedding stuck in the case of that stupid Susan Powter video you gave me. I look like some cheerleader chick posing on the cover of *People* because she took her special needs classmate as a date to prom. You're the only person I know who would actually look better after chemo. Your hair is so fricking stupid. It looks like somebody glued clumps of steel wool all over your head.

October 15, 1999
From: CristElle@hotmail.com
To: Spaho123@hotmail.com
Subject line: u know shit

You know what gets me? U don't even have any idea that Frieda has breast cancer, even after spending all that money on supplements, so she and Jimmy bought some shack in Manzanillo to be close to a holistic healing clinic but I won't be visiting any time soon because tortillas are super fatty and I don't think there's any room for me to sleep. Mindy says he'll probably get executed for drug trafficking down there.

U don't even know that Ivan is leaving. His mom hates Winnipeg so she made his dad take a second horn job in Seattle for her own professional sanity, whatever that means. He said her public relations freelance gig was going nowhere here and she needed an excuse and he thought Winnipeg had an edgy neglected vibe and he wanted to stay put for once. He also said he always envied u and me and I was like, what the fricking hell?

He said it just always seemed like nothing mattered more than CristElle no matter what. What a fricking joke.

October 16, 1999
From: CristElle@hotmail.com
To: Spaho123@hotmail.com
Subject line: blind

U should know Mindy met some balding ginger who drives charter buses and she told me last night that maybe you did what you did out of love. So I told her that number one, her gay-dar sucks, and number two, love must really make u blind because since when was she ready to cut u any kind of slack about this? She's walking around like all is right with the world, humming to herself and dyeing her hair, and mostly I want to punch her in the stomach.

October 16, 1999
From: CristElle@hotmail.com
To: Spaho123@hotmail.com
Subject line: happy ending my skinny ass

U should also know that just because Ivan is buggering off, I'm not lonely, I have other friends. But it's like u really did die and your ghost is haunting me.

Lots of people do that. They talk to their dead loved ones like they're still right there beside them.

Here's the thing. For a while it was like in a movie, except just the happy ending. CristElle was da bomb and everyone was like, whoa! and I got in the choir and I got skinny and everything just kind of fell into place. I had my girls and my fly boyfriend and my gay best friend and everything was peachy. Then u get sick after all the shit you've already been through with that Bosnie fricking war, and here's the really crazy part … things were still really good for me! I was sad, but I was still fricking great!

Which doesn't mean I don't hate you. I meant what I said. It just means you've managed to make me hate myself too. So nice fricking job.

October 17, 1999

I woke up from a dream where Elle was running in a forest and wearing her yellow dress from the wedding but it was all ripped up so you could see the top of her thigh and part of her chest. Since she got skinnier her *grudi* have actually gotten smaller and she calls them her little titties. In my dream she was running to Ivan who was riding a horse and wearing a big furry Cossack hat. They met on the path and he slung her up onto the horse and they rode away to "Can't Help Falling in Love," the UB40 reggae version, and then fancy script wrote out *The End* like in the old movies Baba and Deda Ilić used to show for Wednesday matinees.

Last year I usually woke up with my *kurac* at attention whether I dreamed something or not but during the day it was different. My brain played all kinds of tricks, like maybe Elle was wrong about me and my imagination and I could become one of those gamers who lose their grip on reality and start to think they're more elf than human. When it was gray and ugly outside and it was always the three of us, Elle and Ivan would pretend to argue over something stupid like whether the oboe sounded creepier than the piccolo and then they'd sort of start wrestling on the brown grass and I'd imagine jumping in the middle and all of us making a Cris sandwich, and then I'd have to turn away and imagine something totally different, like massaging Mama's feet before her spring pedicure to get my *kurac* to behave.

October 18, 1999

I can't sleep because I keep thinking about last year, like how Mama talked Dajdža Drago out of getting me the Nintendo for last birthday/Christmas. He handed me a white envelope and said my mama told him I needed an activity. *I think baseball might suit you. Forget the Old World sports. This one's slower and you can follow the statistics and things. One ten-week tutorial at the Dome and you'll be hitting them out of the park.*

Then Amina gave me another envelope with a certificate for private voice lessons, which was a low blow since she knew CristElle was as done as Yugoslavia. And then I started thinking about how things went downhill from there because on Boxing Day the phone rings and Nana Spaho is dead and there's nothing but wailing and arguing for the rest of the week about whether someone should fly home to be the family mourner and who it should be and who should stay home with the boy.

So by the time New Year's came, I guess I was not in the mood for any more noise and walking down into Scottie's stepdad's stuffy rec room, and Scottie on his new drums and Ivan on his new Fender were like the last straw. Only they weren't because Scottie's mom brought down bottles of champagne so we could experiment in a safe environment and it tasted like the fizzy water Tata used to drink when I was small but with an aftertaste of pee. And the girls kept toasting Ivan's new guitar and Ivan and Elle were sitting on the couch like the conjoined twins in our biology textbook.

Then Ivan told everyone about his dad's friend Stan who was an Olympic-caliber skier for the former Czechoslovakia.

Picture this. It's still the Cold War and no one's allowed to leave. But Stan has seen the other side, he knows what freedom looks like. So one night he hikes up to the border, which is guarded with security armed to the teeth. He straps on his skis and races down to Austria in a hail of bullets.

I was sitting on the floor, or that green indoor/outdoor carpet that seems harder than floor, and I told everyone we escaped Sarajevo through an underground tunnel.

Elle sat up then and swatted the top of my head. *You never told me that! I'm his best friend, and he never told me that!* Scottie wanted to know if we were shot at and I said it was hidden underground and one of the girls asked if I was scared shitless and Ivan said, *Aren't you listening? It was secret. The enemy was going about their dumb-ass business up above. Why would he be scared?*

I almost told them about the moths but by then Elle had her head in Ivan's lap and my *kurac* wanted to say Happy New Year! and so I went to the bathroom and spilled out the champagne and stayed there for a while.

October 19, 1999

Elle has been sending emails. For weeks. Amina just told me.

I was dreaming that Budgie was sitting in her usual office chair except in the middle of the tunnel and she was fat like a bird all puffed up to face the cold. I asked Budgie what she was doing there and she said, *Waiting for you to tell me about it* and I said, *Tell you about what?* and she said, *You know.*

Then I opened my eyes because Amina was standing over me, waiting.

How long you going to sleep? I have something to tell you.

Amina said she was looking for Baba's *dolma* recipe in the general family account and she wasn't sure if Mama and Tata just hadn't been checking messages or if they thought it was best for me not to have contact with Elle. I asked her if she'd read them and she said no, which probably wasn't true, and I asked her if Elle still hated me, which is a stupid question, and she said it was not her business and I should read them myself.

But I can't. I can't do it. Even Amina looks at me these days with the same sad eyes as Tata when he decided there was no reason left to stay in his beloved city.

October 21, 1999

This whole week I've been waiting to talk to Budgie because I don't know what else to do. But when she was finally there right in front of me, sort of fidgety and swiveling back and forth in her chair, more like a *ptica* than ever, I just wanted to get out of there.

I never really liked birds, even though I know some of them are pretty smart, like parrots and crows, and I know they're the last surviving dinosaurs. In Sarajevo, Tata used to leave food for the doves on our windowsill and during the siege he complained that there were no more doves, no more songbirds in the trees, but it didn't really bother me. I didn't miss their beady eyes and fidgety necks.

Except I couldn't get up and walk out on Budgie because I'm not an a-hole, and because I had nowhere to go.

I told her I was sorry about her mom and she said it wasn't exactly unexpected, but you can never quite prepare yourself, which reminded me of what Mama and Tata used to say to people about the war. So I told Budgie that you can't believe it until it happens and she said, *My mother was an addict. She was addicted to food and finally her body couldn't take it anymore. I think it's one of the reasons I chose this profession.*

I didn't know what to say, so I told her when Nana Spaho died last year, I barely felt anything. She'd always been old, as long as I could remember. Budgie said she guessed that was the beauty of outliving your generation. *People said my mom was larger than life, in every way. Maybe that's why it's so hard to imagine her gone.*

I told her Tata probably wished Nana Spaho could have lived forever because he let Amina go back with him, and then there was more arguing about which cousin's flat was repaired enough for guests, and what they wanted most in Sarajevo that they still couldn't get in Sarajevo, and how it was all going to fit into the suitcases without going over-weight at baggage check.

He finally told Mama that his mother wouldn't have wanted this, all the cost, all the fuss, and Mama snapped at him the way she usually only snaps at the girls. *You don't want to bury your own mother? What are you afraid of? The fighting's over.* After that Tata shut up pretty much for good.

Budgie wanted to know if I thought he was afraid and I said maybe he was afraid that if he went he might not want to come back, and she said she hadn't thought of that and it was very perceptive of me.

Mama says I have to clear up the dishes from lunch. I want to ask her if she knows about Elle's messages but I'd also rather die than talk about Elle with her. But it's like the more you try not to think about something the more you think about it, like a lame chorus that gets stuck in your head. Sometimes I think Elle is larger than life, even though she's skinny now.

Being with her was like being with the wind.

A few months ago, Mama and Tata got in a big fight after we'd all gone to bed. She called him *a coward who's not willing to face up to the reality of his life.*

October 26, 1999

Budgie said it's been two months and we've come pretty far, made it all the way to 1999. She asked if I was too young to know the song by Prince and I told her it was 1999, they played it everywhere all the time, plus Ivan thought Prince was a *freakzoid genius* and Elle said he was kind of like me, a strange little music man with crazy hair who danced to his own drummer.

When she said it, Ivan was giving her a piggyback and her chin was tucked in his neck but somehow she made it sound like a compliment.

Budgie asked about when Tata and Amina were away and I told her they were supposed to stay in Sarajevo ten days but that was extended because Tata's Aunt Iva, Nana Spaho's half-sister, kept insisting that her apartment stay in the family and it was tricky business. Amina said the building was full of holes, a regular Russian chess field, and Mama explained to me that Chetniks had launched so many random mortars and Russian-supplied rockets that people thought it looked like they were playing tic-tac-toe, or Russian chess. Budgie asked if I was worried they wouldn't come back, and I said no because while they were gone, Ivan went skiing in Quebec with his uncle and it was almost like old times for a while.

Elle came over on the weekend and we made popcorn and watched *Armageddon* and she kept pretending to freak out and I pointed out all the holes in the plot and it was just us talking about the dodgy science and crappy dialogue and how the only female role was "hot young wife."

Then she put her sock feet in my lap like it was the most natural thing in the world. *You know what I keep thinking?*

This is the first time you've been away from Mirza. Like, in your whole life.

I'd never really thought of that, how Tata and I had always been together — before the siege, during the siege, after the siege. He'd never gone anywhere without me.

Elle said that Jimmy would drive her crazy if she saw him every day, and I was going to ask her about it because I'd never thought about that either, how she might miss her dad during those months between visits, only my *kurac* was finally noticing her feet in my lap and so I had to get up for a drink.

Even after Ivan came back in January, Elle still kept coming over like she was worried the apartment would collapse into a black hole without her or Amina around. And Mama was Elle's biggest fan once she looked more like Winona Ryder than Queen Latifah. *It is so good to have you here at this difficult time for our family, Elle. You are such a good girl for our Krysz. Look, I made you his favorite, lepinja. Flatbread is so good no need for butter.*

Budgie wanted to know how I felt and I had an answer for once. Nana Spaho was dead and people were still fighting over her crappy flat but I was happy. I wished things could stay like that forever, or at least the lifespan of a red dwarf star. Just me and Elle like it was before, except with her *lepinja* breath on my neck when she pretended to be scared or the smell of her shampoo in my face when she showed Mama how ticklish I was.

While Tata and Amina were gone, for three weeks, it was as good as the first time I watched *Star Wars* at Baba and Deda Ilić's cinema. I still have no idea where Deda Ilić got his hands on it, that pirated Polish version with Bosnian sub-titles that I couldn't read yet, but it didn't matter.

It was *Star Wars*, and I was in my favorite seat in my second home with my Kakao Krem watching the most crazy exciting thing I'd ever seen in my life.

Budgie smiled, and I was going to tell her that this is the point when the story hits the fan, takes a wrong turn, heads over to the Dark Side. But I just let her smile because the session was pretty much over.

October 27, 1999

I almost read Elle's messages. Now I have to go to the tailor shop with Mama and I've got the shakes. She keeps touching my hair and I want to hit my own mother.

October 28, 1999

Budgie is quitting. After all the *yada-yada-yada*, after all the *chirp-chirp-chirping*, she's decided she needs a holiday. *My colleague Dr. Latinez will meet with you over the next month. I know it's not ideal, Laz-Aaar, but you'll like him. He's been at this for a long time, thirty years. He knows his stuff.*

I couldn't get any words out. After everything, I was going to cry over Budgie?

I'll be back in four weeks. Even doctors need to pause sometimes and see to their own life.

There were tears coming down my face!

I need some time. There are things to settle about my mother, just like your tata had to.

I was watching her skinny little fingers fidgeting in her lap, tearing at a piece of tissue like she hated it, and I was crying.

My daughter, Jessie, is not very verbal. She should be talking more at her age. She needs some testing, Laz-Aaar. And I need to be there. She balled up the tissue in her fist and tried to smile. *I shouldn't be telling you this.*

I am not an a-hole, but I didn't smile back. She got up to get a Kleenex that wasn't all mauled and balled and I told her Elle has been emailing me.

I'm sorry?

She handed me the Kleenex, but I didn't take it and I didn't say it again.

Elle has been writing to you?

Why do people pretend they don't hear you when they do? I am so tired of all the pretending that goes on, day in and day out.

This is the first I've heard of this. What does she say, Laz-Aaar? Let's talk about it. We still have the hour.

Why did you bring it up if you didn't want to talk about it?

I can wait, Laz-Aaar. We have a few more minutes. Let me know when you're ready.

You'll like Dr. Latinez, Laz-Aaar. He was one of my mentors. You should see the waiting list to see him.

It went on like this until time was up and Tata came in his new used car, a 1994 Corolla that Hana's husband got for a song. Tata didn't notice that my eyes were red and there were big fat snowflakes falling on the streets and the tree branches and the fire hydrants. Hana and Sara and Mama hate the winter because of the cold but Tata and I have always liked it. Summer is smelly and noisy and all about growing and thundering and burning. Winter is gray and quiet and all about sleeping like the dead.

Budgie is not the only one who can be patient. I know what it means to wait even when you're young and it doesn't come naturally. They can't make me go see Dr. Grandpa or tell him that I wasn't afraid Tata wouldn't come back from Sarajevo. I was afraid that he would for my sake, and that he'd hate me for it.

I don't have to tell him how tired I am, even though I'm young.

Because I am, I'm tired. I'm tired of trying to figure out the mess and the messages and the *yadda, yadda, yadda, chirp, chirp, chirp.* I'm tired of missing Kakao Krem. I'm tired of imagining what Elle is doing right now.

Because it was only a matter of time before Tata would come home quieter than ever, and Amina would come home louder than ever and Elle would go back to trying to get me to do something with my pot scrubber hair or drag me to sit with them while she snuck fries off Ivan's plate. Valentine's Day would come and Elle would send me a rose from a secret admirer and Amina would help me make Elle *lepinja* with no butter and Ivan would write her a heavy metal knock-off called "Elle's Bells" and Elle would pretend to like them both the same.

Amina would start giving me pep talks again. *You just going to let that arrogant little Russian have her like that? You just going to sit there? What is it with people who sit as if they're helpless? This is a peaceful, free country. You can do as you like. Your destiny isn't dictated by centuries of tribalism and territory.* Mama would start to worry again that I was too skinny, or too pale, or too lazy, and she would take me to the doctor again to see why such a young man should be wasting away and there would be questions and needles and more questions.

How are you feeling these days? Ever feel like it's hard to get out of bed? How about unusual sadness? Do you ever think about hurting yourself? Any thoughts of suicide? Do you have a girlfriend? Are you sexually active? How are your eating habits? What do you do for exercise?

The results would come back inconclusive and Mama would start worrying for real and Tata would finally lose his temper. *Don't be such a foolish woman. He is growing too fast, that's all. You remember what a beanpole I was at his age? It's a stage. Take him back, test him again, you'll see.*

Then more waiting rooms, more doctors, more needles, and I'd start to get how Arman maybe felt after the shrapnel. One day you're a regular little shit in a schoolyard and the next you're under the white lights of the examining room, a superstar of unluckiness because kids shouldn't die. Hana would come home and spend the night because Mama wasn't sleeping, until the second set of tests would come back normal, no problems, perhaps a little depression leading to lethargy.

I don't have to tell Dr. Grandpa that before the siege, whenever Mama worried too much Tata said, *You don't know what trouble is.* Until she really did. Then when she started fretting again here in Canada, Tata couldn't say that to her anymore. All he could say was, *I told you the boy was fine*, and all she could do was stop talking to him.

If Budgie thinks she can pass me off to some other doctor who happens not to be a bird, she's wrong. I can wait. I know how to sit and not think too hard about what's happening to you. I've had practice. And it takes practice, because if you have half a brain thoughts creep in through the cracks.

Like I keep thinking that Ivan and Elle treated me like their kid brother. Sometimes I felt like their kid brother. I was everybody's kid brother.

But other times I felt like they had no idea. They talked big but everything was a game, a laugh, a good story. They had no idea what life could *actually do to you*.

October 30, 1999

In September I made a deal with Mama and Tata. I didn't have to start grade eleven right away if I went to the doctor. Now mama is saying since I'm not going to the doctor, then I have to go to school. So I took off and slept in Scottie Abrams' garage, which I remembered is heated because his dad loves cars more than people. I came back to the apartment just as the police were leaving, and Mama hugged me like it had been one year instead of one night, then cuffed me on the ear and cried and held my hands and asked what they were going to do with me as if I might have any idea.

Tata said nothing and later Mama made *lepinja*, which doesn't remind me of my childhood anymore.

It reminds me of Elle.

Sara moved into a townhouse with her friend from work last week. Amina came into my room yesterday and threw a paper airplane at my head. It was a copy of her old Siege of Sarajevo flyer, the one she spent so much time laying out on our crap computer and then printing and photocopying and never really handing it out to anyone but us.

Read it, she said, *because even if you were in school, you wouldn't be learning this shit.* After that she took off for Toronto, then Frankfurt, then Belgrade, then Sarajevo.

Mama and Tata are busy pretending the other one isn't there.

It's winter in here.

December 7, 1999

It's possible to sleep fourteen hours a day and still be tired. I learned that as a kid. It's possible to stare at a crack in the window glass until the sunlight plays tricks on you, turns everything out the window and inside the kitchen into colored blobs with no meaning. Like when you rub your eyes, close them hard and let the light dance across the darkness.

It's possible to hear your own heart beating the way it has since you were inside your mama, to hear your blood pulsing up your arteries, swooshing around your head, draining back down your veins like a soundtrack to that diagram in biology class.

After Nana Spaho died, Elle put her bare feet in my lap once and closed her eyes and I traced the branches of blue veins on the top of her feet with my finger. She asked me to tell her fortune and I said stupid things like, *You will seek your fame closer to home than some think. You will live longer than most. You will marry someone from exotic lands.*

But I didn't tell Budgie any of this. I only went back because I heard Mama and Tata talking again about maybe hauling me off to the loony bin.

Budgie let her hair grow out a bit and it was kind of curly around her shoulders. She also changed it to the wheat blonde that Sara had as a kid even though she turned out to be just as dark as the rest of us.

Budgie said I didn't look so hot and asked if I'd been sleeping. Then she said it was good to see me again.

Maybe we should just try and pick up things where we left them. Do you want to tell me about Elle's messages?

I told her there was nothing to tell.

Okay. Last time we talked about last winter with Elle, when it was just like old times.

Yeah, I wanted to say. I may be crazy, but my short-term memory is just fine. Elle and I. Last winter. Just like old times, but better.

You will be loved by many and envy may haunt you. You will be betrayed by someone close to you.

Budgie touched my knee with her little birdie claw. *Then things changed, Laz-Aaar. That's where we're at.*

I know this is where it gets hard, Laz-Aaar. But this is why we're here.

Would you like another doctor, Laz-Aaar? We can do that, you know. It doesn't have to be me. I know my absence came at a hard time.

I don't know why I didn't end it there. I could have. She said so.

What makes us keep coming back for more? How can Tata keep missing something so much when he knows it's as dead as the dodo? How can Amina keep harping on about justice, about dreaming big, when she knows she will never get what she wants?

All I know is that I started telling Budgie about Dajdža Drago like my brain had been on deep freeze and her *chirp-chirp-chirping* was the spring.

I told her he had the heart attack after Valentine's Day, right when he and Sharon were landing from their vacation in Thailand. Sharon didn't call Mama until the next day and things went downhill from there. Dajdža Drago hit his head when he collapsed in the airplane aisle and the whole time they waited for him to regain consciousness in the hospital Mama and Sharon couldn't agree on anything. Sharon started talking with the doctors about *options,* and

Mama said it was a betrayal to talk about anything other than hope, and Tata was in between, suddenly as talkative as Ivan after a can of Coke in the morning.

All of us were jammed into that little private hospital room and Tata told them to be kind to each other for the sake of the man they both loved. He kept repeating to them what the doctor actually said. He reminded Mama of the letters Dajdža Drago used to send home about this amazing Sharon. He did everything but handstands to keep them from killing each other. Maybe his brother-in-law was finally quiet enough to let him get a word in edgewise.

Budgie smiled, and I told her I remember I was just so tired and Mama said it was because I wasn't eating enough meat, but all I could think of was how Dajdža Drago looked in that hospital bed and how much I wanted to be him, so clueless and limp and peaceful. Everyone was talking like Dajdža Drago wasn't an overbearing *seronja* but the king of kindness and generosity. Even Tata.

All the guy had to do was lie there, brain dead, and he was suddenly a hero.

Mindy always said people can't appreciate what they have until it's taken away, but then the memory of how it was becomes like a movie trailer of the best bits. Budgie wanted to know how so, and I said just look at Sarajevo.

If you weren't a little kid caged inside like a guinea pig, if you were actually out there fighting for your life and hating your mortal enemy, it was the opposite of boring. Even if you weren't a drama queen like Amina, even if the whole thing was your biggest nightmare, you maybe never felt so alive and afterwards nothing else could really compare. And maybe that's why you want to see the past as a kind of hyped-up version of how it was because that's how trailers work. The announcer comes on over an aerial view of Sarajevo and some major guitar chords play and the announcer says something like *Once upon a time, in a galaxy far, far away, there was a valley city of harmony and peace among religions and peoples.*

Budgie wasn't smiling anymore. Her beaky nostrils were kind of flared out, almost like she was trying not to cry. It was not a flattering look, as Elle would say, and I pretended not to notice. I told her when the doctors finally pulled the plug on Dajdža Drago, Mama and Sharon moved on to arguing about where he should be buried. Mama said it would kill her poor ailing parents in Serbia if he was not buried "back home" and Sharon said Canada is his home, not some war-ravaged cauldron of racial hatred and so on.

In the end Mama won, maybe because coming from a war-ravaged cauldron of racial hatred makes you tougher.

By the end of February she and Tata and Sharon and Dajdža Drago's body-in-a-box were on their way to Belgrade and Sara moved back into the apartment to make sure I didn't burn the place down. She was not happy to be there and I wasn't exactly happy either so we mostly minded our own business.

Budgie asked if my parents were hesitant to go back because wasn't it just last spring when NATO began its attacks against Serbia? I told her Mama convinced Sharon that the Western powers talked big but they'd have Dajdža Drago long buried before the UN or NATO would raise a stink about Serbia attacking its own little province of Kosovo. Which was true enough for Sharon, who got the hell out of her in-law's clutches before NATO bombed the Chinese

Embassy and the Ministry of Defence and the radio tower got blown to bits.

All I knew was that Mama winning that war with Sharon and ending up stuck in Belgrade was the first nail in my fake coffin.

The next was Elle catching up with me on the way home from school. I remember it was March 1st and still -22 C with the wind chill, and we were walking fast and talking into our parka collars, which is a stupid way to have a conversation.

She asked if I was okay because I looked like shit and I said, *Thanks.*

No, I mean you look pale.

It's March. Everyone's pale.

No, I mean more than usual. And you're so skinny.

I thought skinny was good.

You know what I mean. More than usual.

Whatever.

Okay, you don't have to be an ass. I'm just worried about you.

I'm just freezing. There's icicles in my chest.

How can you be such a suck, Cris? I thought you were a Winter Olympics baby.

She knew perfectly well that there is cold and then there is *cold* and Sarajevo barely ever dips below -5 C. But she never used to act all worried about me and I started to wonder if maybe I wasn't okay. Mama had shown Dr. Mustafa a bruise on my hip and he'd frowned and made a low humming noise. I was pretty sure it was from walking into a desk following Elle out of math class but then he asked about other bruises and there were two small ones on my biceps we couldn't figure out.

That's when he said we should check my blood to rule out abnormalities such as leukemia, and that's when Mama started checking off boxes. *Yes, his appetite is bad. Yes, he is sleepy. Yes, he keeps getting colds.*

And so I started to wonder. The second set of results said everything was okay but sometimes they made mistakes, didn't they?

Then it all came spilling out like that old slapstick scene where someone's shoved way too much junk in a closet and then someone else opens the door. I told her I think maybe a part of me actually believed it was true.

I told Budgie how I went to the library and looked up the kind of leukemia most teenagers get and made a checklist of other symptoms that I was suffering from or maybe had suffered from. Before the mid-term English exam I got sores in my mouth. I had diarrhea every time I came home from Dajdža Drago's. When the temperature dipped below -25 C sometimes I had *dyspnea*, or trouble breathing.

I made myself believe, at least for a while. For a while it was like the only thing that made me feel like getting up in the morning was the fact I might be dying.

Budgie said I was on my own and the lonely mind does amazing things to survive.

If Elle was there, she would have said that was the biggest fricking pile of BS she'd ever heard.

December 9, 1999

Budgie looked at me and said, *You haven't been sleeping.* A couple of months ago I would have wondered if she was reading my mind but that was before I knew she was just Budgie, with her addict mom and retarded daughter who doesn't talk. Elle gets mad at Ivan when he says something is retarded because it's ignorant and offensive, but he says she's ignorant because the word is now divorced from actual people, who are now referred to as special needs.

Either way I guess I'm an a-hole for writing that about Budgie's kid, except I wonder if it's still offensive if you only say it to yourself.

Budgie said she has used sleep aids herself and would prescribe me something if I was still having trouble next week. Apparently it was tricky sometimes to find something that would make me not too sleepy and not too awake and it might take some time to figure out what worked best.

I said I guess it's just like magic cloaks or magic wardrobes, there are no magic pills. And she might think that I had some big plan for what I did but I didn't. Amina said that from the moment Slobodan Milošević turned his back on trying to fill Tito's giant Yugoslav shoes, he never went off script preaching the story of tragic downtrodden Serbs rising up like phoenixes out of the ashes of their country. Maybe he believed in that just like my Deda Ilić believed in the Orthodox Jesus. But I didn't even believe enough to have a plan.

Tell me about how it started, Budgie said.

I told her Ms. Gulliani chose *Joseph and the Amazing Technicolor Dreamcoat* for the spring musical and Elle said any show that starred plastic-haired big-toothed Donny

Osmond on Broadway probably wasn't worth our time. Plus they always give the lead role to someone in grade twelve.

I didn't think any of us were trying out for a part until Ivan told me they'd picked him to be Joseph.

But where were you, Cris? You could've handed me my ass on a platter.

Then it just came out.

I've got some health stuff going on.

Then, as the classes changed in the music room.

Acute lymphoblastic leukemia. Ongoing anemia…. dyspnea and pallor. Quarts of blood … bone marrow exams … lymph node biopsy.

Wait. Are you telling me you have cancer?

Chemo course of vincristine, doxorubicin and cytarabine. Possible bone marrow transplant.

Cris, holy shit. I had no idea.

I just found out.

Holy shit, Cris.

Don't tell anyone.

Don't tell anyone? You're going to need support, dude. We're here for you.

I can still hear Ivan saying *dude*, hear the class buzzer going off like an air raid siren.

Just like that, I was back in a place where all bets are off and how things will end is anybody's guess.

I signed myself out at the office and I went home and puked up my lunch and hoped it was another sign that maybe the blood tests had lied and not me.

After school Elle showed up and it was like she couldn't decide whether to punch me in the face or hug me until I couldn't breathe.

Why didn't you tell me? All this time I've been asking how you are and I have to find out from somebody else? You make me crazy. We've been best friends for how long? And sometimes you act like you're off in la-la Crislandia and you don't even give a shit. This is serious, Cris. You can't do this alone. We love you and you can't shut us out. We're going to fight this together every step of the way.

She wanted to know where Mama and Tata were, why I was by myself in the apartment when I looked like I might keel over any moment and I told her they were both at work. I didn't tell her about Dajdža Drago's corpse on a plane or Tata needing to go so Mama and Sharon didn't kill each other or Sara moving back in but spending all her waking hours at her friend Bianca's condo with the fitness facility.

I've been trying to figure out why I didn't tell her and all I can think of is, lies are maybe like cancer cells, spreading just for the heck of it. It's like the first one goes rogue and takes on a life of its own and then the rest keep going because they can't help it, they're cancer cells and that's what they do.

Because after she calmed down, Elle took me to the couch and she made me put my head in her lap and she ran her fingers through my hair, the pot-scrubber she hated so much and that I would probably lose soon anyway. She told me she was skipping her visit to Jimmy's this spring so she could be there for me, and Mindy was already buying a frozen lasagna to bring over because knowing Mama she was probably in no state to cook. Then she sang Cher's "Believe," except for the second verse because she couldn't remember it.

Ms. Champagne called me in the next day and said not to worry about my classes, especially math, we would work at my pace, see how things went, and I must, I absolutely must, let her know at any time if there was anything, *anything at all*, that the school could do to make things easier. Guys who never even looked at me before held up a fist in the hall and said, *Stay strong, man*. Amanda-P started carrying my backpack and praying for me.

Before Budgie could ask, I told her.

I said I was thinking, that whole spring, it wasn't like old times. It wasn't like watching *Star Wars* in our old cinema.

It was like a wild and crazy dream that you can't wake up from because you don't want to.

December 10, 1999

Amina just phoned and wanted to talk to me but I didn't feel like it. She told Mama that Ratko Mladić, the fatherless tinsmith turned general who ordered the siege of Sarajevo, was still hiding out but it was only a matter of time before they found him and hauled his ass to the war crimes tribunal in some Dutch place called the Hague.

Mama said that it was shameful I wouldn't come out of my room to talk to my own sister.

I think maybe with a name like Ratko you don't stand much chance of becoming one of the good guys.

December 13, 1999

Budgie says your life is like a story but I didn't dream up being a kid in a war. I always thought a story is when you imagine things like in English class, the way Mr. Wenzel and Ivan got each other off talking about fairytales and myths and the heroic journey. Last year I asked Elle what *get each other off* meant and then she wouldn't shut up about my face getting as red as Wenzel's shirt.

But my question is, where do heroic journeys end and lies start?

I can't sleep and thoughts are pouring into my brain like a soaker in April. The first time my runner filled up with ice-cold muck when we were crossing the track field Elle said, *You're not a real Canadian until you've had your first soaker.*

But I haven't thought about our time in the mall this past spring at all. Not once. I couldn't. Or I wouldn't. Only now I can't stop.

Because during spring break, after I shaved my head, I had to keep Elle out of the apartment in case Sara dropped in. So I told her the one thing she could do was help me escape from Mama's sniveling. I told her the chemo made me kind of weak and dizzy and maybe we could hang out with Mindy's collection of small appliance boxes and Beta-max movies with no Beta machine to play them in.

But then Mindy got a wheelchair from a friend at work whose husband died from some muscle-wasting disease. Except it was March and the melt and freeze left big slushy ice ruts everywhere. So we ended up hanging out with the fast food and fake plants at Polo Park.

And now it's all playing in my head like a movie stuck in its montage scene.

Elle is eating in the food court with me because life is too short to treat celery as more than a chewing exercise. She has two fries hanging from her upper lip like tusks and is waving her arms like walrus flippers to make me laugh until Coke comes out of my nose. She is holding my hand and finger-painting little stripes of make-up tester, trying to find one that will make me look less scary pale but not trashy fake tan. She is standing in front of the wall of magazines at Shoppers Drug Mart and reaching for a magazine that says America's Sweetheart Julia Roberts might be getting back together with pit-faced singer Lyle Lovett. There is a gap between her jeans and her T-shirt and I hold her steady by putting my hand on the bare skin where her waist curves and she laughs like it tickles. We are waiting for the elevator with the grumpy moms pushing strollers and grumpy old ladies pushing walkers and Elle is massaging my bald head and my ear lobes and my temples and everyone is staring at us but we don't care. It's still March so I'm wearing a jacket and no one sees that my *kurac* isn't bothered by the chemo.

It all keeps coming, blending one into the other while Ali Campbell's smooth reggae vocals keep telling me what wise men say. Elle is sitting on my lap as we roll down the perfectly clean tiles of the not-too-hot not-too-cold mall and she is not noticing that I suddenly have strength enough for both of us.

—

The thing is I think Elle maybe liked pushing me around in that folding wheelchair. When we first met she told me teachers were always cutting her slack because she was the bastard child of an absent stoner and a scatterbrained pack-rat. She said people felt sorry for her fatty self and since I was a sad-sack refugee we were a good match.

But later when she started to look like the daughter in a commercial where the whole family sits down together to eat frozen pizza that tastes like delivery, that wasn't true any-more. Like how you look can actually change how you are.

Only maybe it's like they say, old habits die hard, and maybe she kind of missed her old sad-sack self. Because I swear, she loved to talk about how we were battling this cancer together. At the mall, she was always talking about my diagnosis to some mom pushing her crying baby in the elevator or some old guy nursing the same cup of coffee for the second hour in a row. She told our teachers more about my treatments than I did. They were my lies, but she was the one who polished them and spread them and made them her own.

Ivan was the opposite. After that first day, after he told Elle and my fate was sealed, he would come up to me in the hallway sometimes and just stand there looking like a little kid who'd lost his parents in the grocery store. Then he'd ask me how I was holding up and I'd tell him, *Taking it day by day* and he'd shake his head and say, *How do you do it, dude?*

It was kind of creepy to see Ivan at a loss for words.

—

Elle and I are at the Cineplex watching *She's All That*, the one where the handsome jock's friends dare him to ask out the icky brainiac girl, and Elle keeps whispering in my ear, *Do they think we're stupid … That girl is not ugly … That girl was never ugly … They stuck some big glasses on a fricking fashion model … What a crock of horseshit.* The guy behind us is telling her to shut up and she is hissing back at him, *He has cancer, shitface. Leave us alone.*

Elle and I are in the back of Mindy's crappy car and she was up late last night after some choir event I skipped due to "fatigue" so her head drops on my shoulder and her nose is slightly stuffed and so there is a little whistling sound when I touch those soft hairs at the back of her neck and she pretends she doesn't notice but I know she does.

You do something and things happen because of it. Or things happen and you do something because of it. And sometimes you lose track of the difference between the two and before you know it life isn't a story, it's a perfect storm.

So I tell Sara I'll be out a lot doing sound for the school musical and she tells me I look like a concentration camp survivor with my head shaved but she eats up my lie like it's a maple donut and goes on her way because she's more normal than the rest of us. Elle says Hana tries too hard and Amina doesn't try at all, but from the minute we got here Sara was a regular old Canadian.

Then Mama calls from Belgrade to say Deda Ilić has vascular dementia and she has to stay and move the stubborn *dete* into some place where he'll get the care he needs and I tell her the same thing, that I'll be busy with the musical. And she believes me too, because she has no choice.

What I want to know is, would things have gone on so long if someone had been there to stop me?

December 14, 1999

Elle and I are sitting up front by the driver in the area reserved for the baby strollers and disabled people. She is
sweaty from pushing me across the street at a run to catch
the bus and elbows me in the face when she takes off her
scarf. I laugh even though it hurt and she wraps the scarf
around my bald head like my Deda Ilić used to when he
had a toothache. It's the same butter yellow as the dress she
wore to Hana's wedding. The guy across from us is blind
and we watch his poor guide dog, who wants to sit down
and take a load off, stand there obediently because the bus
floor is covered in about an inch of grit and snow slop.

Don't leave me, okay, Elle says, and I am going to tell her,
but then our stop comes.

Ivan's musical practice is canceled at the last minute and
we're at Mindy's watching *Blast from the Past* where the
Brendan Fraser character grows up in an underground
bomb shelter, then comes out when he's thirty years old
and has to try and figure out modern-day LA. *That's what
Cris was like when he came to Canada,* Elle says, and Ivan
expects me to be offended but I'm not because the guy,
whose name is Adam, gets Alicia Silverstone in the end.
Also Ivan is acting like a beach ball with a slow leak, still
round but without much bounce.

Amanda-P tells me that my name was on her church bul-
letin's prayer list and Elle points out that my family were
practicing Tito Communists who believed blind faith in an

afterlife distracts the masses from fighting oppression here and now. I guess she got this from Amina, but Amanda-P looks like she's going to cry and so we do a group hug, with me as the middle of the sandwich.

I buzz up to Mindy's apartment and when Elle comes down I throw a fistful of snow in her face and then outside we're scooping up slush in our bare hands and throwing it at each other like kids splashing in a pool. We end up on the ground and I am sweeping the wet hair from her eyes, which are river-at-sunset brown against the gray snow, and I almost tell her.

But she scrambles to her feet and says it's not good for me to get all cold and wet like this.

We're on the risers during choir practice. Elle is behind me and runs her pointer finger down the notches of my spine.

You know what I hate? she whispers. *Here's my list. Country-western crossover pop singers. The sound of people talking German. Sourpusses. Rice pudding. Fakers. Humidity. Leukemia. I officially now hate leukemia more than anything.*

I almost tell her, but some a-hole has asked Ivan to sing Joseph's big song, "Any Dream Will Do."

December 15, 1999

I've been adding it up and I betrayed CristElle over and over. Not just three, like Peter the disciple. I was thinking about Deda Ilić and the picture Bible he gave me without telling Mama and Tata. The one with the painting of Abraham ready to stab his son to prove his faith, or Judas standing behind Jesus like a mafia gangster at the last supper. But the one that bothered Deda Ilić most was the one of Peter looking not really sad, but more like surprised. Deda said it was because he couldn't believe what he'd just done to his hero.

December 16, 1999

Budgie wanted to know how I've been sleeping and I said okay because I didn't want her to bring up pills again. Elle said I have an *irrational aversion to mind-altering chemicals* but this is coming from someone who got high at her dad's when she was thirteen. She said she was glad that she didn't really like it because who knows, she might have an addictive personality and I said all I know is that before the war Bosnian Serbs and Croats and Muslims always got along until they were drunk.

Budgie said I didn't look like I'd been sleeping okay and I told her that I'd been thinking that as long as I had cancer everything was better than great and worse than terrible at the same time. And maybe that's how the Serbs felt when they knew they had this dream but first they had to destroy everything.

You've been thinking a lot, Laz-Aaar, Budgie said. She was wearing a creamy beige shirt that matched her new hair. I told her the whole time I kept saying to myself, *Okay, this is it, this will be the day the craziness ends.* But now I think even Milošević, with all his speeches and waving of the Serbian flag, didn't know it would lead to ten years of war crimes. Once these things get going they take on a life of their own.

All through April, Ivan is still off practicing for his stage debut and Mindy says Elle is a better nurse than she would have guessed in a zillion years and Mama keeps phoning to assure me they're safe and giving me updates on how Milošević is kicking all the poor Albanians out of Kosovo, which is all over the news and I don't even care about it, and senile Deda Ilić who I don't even feel sorry for because

I keep thinking that sometimes losing your mind can be a good thing especially when you're old and your world is gone. I felt almost jealous because I was still young and the world was waiting, only I'd decided to light things up and watch things burn.

So April turns to May and Mama and Tata finally book their flights home and the flames start spreading out of control. They're an inferno licking the sky and I'm not cut out for that kind of heat.

I don't tell Budgie this last crazy bit. I told her when I told Elle I was feeling too weak to go to opening night of *Joseph and the Amazing Technicolor Dreamcoat* she called me a crappy friend because all I had to do was sit there.

Ivan reserved front row seats for us, which sounds good, but for a Broadway kind of musical all you see is feet. Part of Scottie's beard wasn't glued on right and kept flapping in the dance numbers and Amanda-P was way too excited up there to be playing one of The Wives.

When the curtain finally closed, the parents gave a standing ovation and when the clapping was done, Ivan came out by himself and pulled off his hair.

But it wasn't his hair, it was a wig. He was completely bald and he said the night's proceeds would be donated to Cris Spaho, who was *heroically engaged in the fight of his life*. He called me up to the stage and Elle made me go and she came with me and she kept kissing Ivan's head, which was kind of flat at the back. *Holy shit, Ivy! I can't believe it! You are amazing! All your beautiful hair! And Cris almost didn't come! Can you believe that? He almost didn't come!*

Budgie waited for me to keep going. But I was suddenly so tired it felt like my mouth was full of socks. She asked how I felt about what Ivan did, and I told her it was like he was so alive that he was too good for pesky old death. And in the end him shaving his head and thinking to donate the musical money, all that was more about him than me.

Budgie asked if I wanted to know what she thought, like she could see how tired I was. *I think generosity is almost never pure, or selfless. It's up to each of us to look hard at ourselves and then decide how to be a good person. Some of us get it right, some never do. Most of us just keep trying.*

I waited, because I was so tired.

And you know what growing up is? It's figuring out how to think about someone other than yourself. That's basically it.

I said I thought it was just getting hairy in your privates and she laughed like we were old friends sharing a beer.

December 17, 1999

Hana used to say that I could sleep through anything, that I wouldn't notice if a meteorite hit the apartment next door, but now it's like everything wakes me up.

My *kurac* was at half attention because I was dreaming of Elle except she was still as *debeo* as when we met, and it got me wondering about Fat Elle and Skinny Elle. She always said that I was the only person who didn't give two shits about her weight and I always thought she was right, only now I'm thinking the truth is never that simple no matter how many times Elle or Budgie say it is.

I think maybe Fat Elle, the one who made me go swimming and who was going to be a pop star, she let herself eat all the junk she wanted because she thought she deserved to eat all the junk she wanted. And maybe Skinny Elle, the one who looked like Annie Lennox's little sister, she cared about who showed up at her birthday party because she thought everyone should love her. I think they're both just Elle to me, but what I want to know is does my *kurac* care. I never thought of her that way when she was *debeo* and maybe not just because we were kids because I know during the siege my kid *kurac* noticed things sometimes.

Like one time Hana thought I was asleep with everyone else when Goran, who used to sweep the floors in the cinema, snuck in from the balcony. The streetlights hadn't been on for weeks but the moon was big and bright and the muscles in his arms were strained from climbing up three stories. It was like he was trying to devour Hana's tongue and I knew I should turn around and go back to sleep, but I didn't. I watched them sucking and licking at each other while Hana said, *You coulda died, you coulda died,* and my *kurac* came to life even though Goran could have died. And I never really felt like that again until the first time I saw Ivan and Skinny Elle wrapped up together like a pretzel. So maybe my *kurac* does care.

Maybe it only wants the Elle who only wanted me if I was dying.

December 18, 1999

I just remembered something. Hana's sweeper, Goran, he was there the night we left through the tunnel. We had to sit for what seemed like days, crowded on top of each other in that stuffy little garage dressed up like an old lady's sitting room, waiting with all our bags and boxes and packs, while Baba Sida, who once owned the house, kept trying to hand me a ball of old bread. *We ate,* Tata kept telling her. *Save it for a hungry soldier.* By the time we finally got the A-OK and gathered up our stuff and trudged through what she called her garden because I guess stuff grew there once, I was so happy to be moving I would have followed that line of people straight into a pack of hungry wolves or a rushing mudslide or a hail of bullets — as long as it meant we didn't have to wait anymore.

I overheard Tata and his friends gossip about the tunnel all the time. The Dobrinja side was shored up by metal from bombed-out Sarajevo factories but the Butmir side used wood from Mount Igman. The whole thing was taken over for a while by black market thieves smuggling alcohol and stolen UN packages.

I got it in my head that it must be really big like a railway tunnel through a mountain, maybe because that's the only kind of tunnel I'd seen. When I was five, I overheard the girls talking about how babies come through a tunnel between a woman's legs and I imagined Mama with a little tiny cupboard door down there that the doctor opened to let me out.

So maybe I'm just not good at imagining things I haven't seen with my own eyes.

But really the tunnel was nothing more than a narrow cellar like in the traditional farmhouse we visited once for school, just tall enough for a kid like me to stand. This one just happened to be dug into what once was Baba Sida's kitchen and kept going for 800 meters.

Maybe I was the only one who noticed Goran because I wasn't carrying as much. Tata told Mama and the girls over and over to take less stuff and they were determined to make it seem like it was not a problem. They could wear a heavy pack and drag a heavy bag while bent for two hours in the damp. Maybe Sara and Mama were already struggling down the stairs trying not to huff or slip or look back when I saw him off to the side out of line whispering to his mother, who was teetering on the edge of a wheelbarrow, shaking her head like a two-year-old who doesn't want to take a bath. *I can't,* she said. *I can't breathe.*

Only as I followed Tata down I could still hear Goran's voice, the last voice I heard in Sarajevo. *Maaaa, be reasonable. It's perfectly safe. Maaaa.* The next thing I really remember is hurrying across the tarmac and the wind blowing my hair in crazy directions and the sky above the mountains turning dusky blue, a light soft enough to touch as Baba used to say. My whole family remembers the wind and Mama doing up my seatbelt because I was asleep before the plane took off.

But Goran, and the sky, they're all my own, and I have no idea if I just imagined them. Maybe the whole thing with Goran and Hana in the moonlight was my first perverted wet dream about my own sister.

—

Mama just got off the phone with Baba in Belgrade and started crying like she believed the predictions were right and the world would end in a couple of weeks. Tata told her that her father wasn't the first old man to forget what his wife looks like and he wouldn't be the last, so she should get a hold of herself for pity's sake. She even came into my room and sat down on the bed and talked in Bosnian even though I was pretending to be asleep. *When will it end, son? That's all I want to know. Because I was not prepared for this, you know. My girlhood was unusually blessed. Maybe too blessed. I used to think I was a strong person. Stronger than your father and his numbers and his loneliness. But no one told me life would be this pitiless.*

I kept my breathing slow and even, even gave a little twitch, but she didn't stop. *My mother, the dearest of mothers, should not have to go through this alone. She said the only one he seems to recognize is one of the food servers, some girl with freckles on her chest and crooked teeth. He calls for Filipa, where is Filipa? He wants to tell her again about his sister, Anka, how she died fifteen years ago from ovarian cancer that the doctor had misdiagnosed as irritable bowels. Can you imagine?*

And I realized I can imagine, I can, because for the last while I have been losing my mind as fast as poor Deda Ilić in that old Belgrade care home that Amina says was a historic building but now has nothing but drips and drafts. Just like Deda Ilić I barely notice my own mama and tata tiptoeing around me. Since I sat down with Budgie, since I started filling these pages, it's like the past is more real than the present, like some bird lady who has her own problems is more important than my own family.

If I were there he would know me, son. He used to call me his slatki because he had such sweet-tooth just like you. You both like the candy and the movies and the romantic songs. It's like you are both too soft for this hard world.

I let her go on, talking over her son who wished he was old and senile or better yet a corpse but was only a ghost who happened to be alive.

Until I think even she got tired of her own voice and left me alone.

I never thought birthdays could get much worse than during a siege, but maybe they can, because I turn sixteen in less than a week. I wish I could go back and tell that little Luke Skywalker wannabe to chase his dog across a checkpoint and get shot in the head. That happened to a boy in '92 and Amina told Mama they just named a park after him.

I'm not sure I really want to die. I would miss some things like music and math and missing Elle. It's just I'm so tired of being a ghost and no matter how much I *yadda-yadda-yadda*, no matter how much I think, I'm still too afraid to read Elle's messages because then maybe that will be it. I'll want to die.

December 19, 1999

I spent the last few hours trying to not remember anything. I watched some *Law and Order: Special Victims Unit* with Mama, and she was so excited it made me feel like an a-hole. Tata came and asked her how she could watch that Hollywood violence after what we'd witnessed ourselves in the flesh and she just ignored him. She's getting a bit of a bulgy stomach, the kind that make old ladies like Baba look a little pregnant even though that's impossible. She kept scraping nail polish off with her teeth while the beautiful detective kept discovering more female prisoners who'd been raped and tortured, maybe by their prison guard.

Mama hasn't been making me go to the tailor shop because she hasn't been working there as much. She said Amina isn't coming back from Sarajevo for the holidays and Hana is spending the day with her in-laws and Sara is going to Cuba with a friend so there's no point in putting up a tree. The only sign that it's Christmas in here are cards on the TV with snowy Bosnian mountains or Orthodox cathedrals with nativity scenes.

Turns out though that Tata has started working for some guy named Farik, another Bosnian refugee who's trying to start his own drafting business. And he's tutoring Farik's son in math because he only has a B average and wants to be an aeronautical engineer, which Tata thinks is a long shot. He told me that mastering calculus requires a certain kind of brain wiring which Hana and I both have but Sara and Amina don't.

December 21, 1999

Budgie was wearing a top and pants that were attached and kind of looked like pajamas. She seemed like a kid waiting for her bedtime story.

During the siege I knew I was getting too old for stories and I knew it was hard for Mama but I made her keep telling me the one where an American actor stars in a detective show and then starts solving mysteries on the side. One time she said, *Not tonight, my Krysztof. Please don't make me do it. Please, if you love me you won't ask again,* and I felt bad because I was a kid but I wasn't an a-hole.

Budgie asked if I'd read Elle's messages yet and I wanted to say, *Please, if you love me, you won't ask again.* Except I know Budgie doesn't love me. I'm just a patient. I asked if she wanted to hear how it all ended because I don't know what Mama and Tata told her and they didn't know much anyway and she said, *Yes, whatever you like.*

If life was a movie maybe I would have rushed up on stage when Ivan gave me the proceeds from the musical and said the joke was on him. I lied. I didn't have cancer and he'd shaved off his Johnny Depp hair for nothing.

But instead I shook his hand and let him rub my scalp like I was a good dog and posed for a picture and tried to look as sick as I felt.

Budgie uncrossed her legs and leaned forward with her elbows on her knees and I noticed that her outfit really pulled in the crotch area. I also noticed she didn't have her wedding ring on anymore and I must have sat there for a while because she finally said, *The school called your mom.*

So Mama had told her about the phone call from the

office saying the check was ready for me to pick up, about the school secretary telling Mama the story of her sister's husband's cousin who beat leukemia but unfortunately died of liver failure three years later. About how Mama thought we'd hidden my cancer from her because one woman can only take so much.

Budgie already knew that with one phone call I went from hero to hell.

I told her maybe I did need something to help me sleep. She put her hand on mine like when Jesus touches the leper in Deda Ilić's picture Bible.

I know this is tough stuff, Laz-Aaar.

It's hard to say what it feels like because it's not really a feeling. It's more like an out-of-body experience like in the movies when someone's soul shows up to check out their own funeral only in this case you're not dead. You're still talking out of your same old mouth, still seeing out of your same old eyes, still needing to open a door to get out of a room. But you're off to the side watching the one who came up with the lies, who let it go on, who didn't even try to get out of the trap he'd made.

Cris the Crazy has not just lost his very own cinema to the Dark Side. He has not just lost Elle to Ivan. He's lost everything and it's all his fault. And yet he keeps going! He goes to Giesbrecht the guidance counselor who looks more scared than Cris the Crazy because this is his first year on the job and all he's had to deal with so far is stuff like vandalism and truancy and family break-ups. So Cris the Crazy ends up spending the last few weeks of school at home in his room, on the waiting list to see the kind of doctor who deals with what Elle calls *bonafide wack jobs*.

Budgie squeezed my hand a little too hard and I closed my eyes. There was still a faded tan line where her ring should have been.

I know Elle said some harsh things.

Mama told her that too. How I waited forever for Elle to come and let me have it like only she could and then I waited some more. She didn't come until Canada Day, when we were all invited over to Hana's new house because it was only right that we show our pride as new Canadians. It was a Dajdža Drago-style party with AAA Canadian beef and homemade Canadian butter tarts and Canadian beer and I said I felt like I was going to throw up and Tata said he would stay with me but somehow it was Mama who was there when Elle came.

I was lying on my bed with a hot water bottle and maybe Mama listened at the door because Elle didn't shout or even talk loud. She was wearing a blue tank top that probably came out of the bottom of the laundry pile and white shorts that seemed a little tight. She just stared down at me waiting, and it was like my voice had gone to Hana's barbecue and left me here. I had to close my eyes.

What the hell, Cris?

I remember her bra straps were bright yellow. Blue and yellow. Like the Bosnian flag.

Really? You have nothing to say? Are you serious?

She sort of whispered it and she was crying a little, and all I could think of was how small she looked, how breakable compared to my old Elle.

You are dead to me. You are more than dead to me. It's like you never came here. You were never born, Cris. Do you hear me? You never existed.

I've never been sure if quicksand really exists except in the movies. You don't read about a lot of quicksand deaths in the paper. But that's when I knew how landing in a pit of quicksand must feel. You're falling and falling and you think you've hit bottom until the ground shifts and swallows you whole.

December 22, 1999

I slept until eleven thanks to Budgie's pills. I'm still not quite awake but I still keep thinking about something Amina wrote for the *Free Press*. Tata clips every story that's published and keeps a file under the phone book.

The civilized people of Sarajevo waited patiently for the world to step in and help them help themselves — but the world arrived too late.

Anger and bitterness and fear had already won the day. Ordinary young people were ready to get rich by stealing bread from children. Ordinary old people were ready to kill. Even shy math teachers were willing to beg, borrow and steal to get their families out.

Can you blame the wasted people of Sarajevo if they came to hate the impotent UN nearly as much as their enemies?

I thought sleeping would make me less tired, but I was wrong.

I could hear Sara and Mama watching the *Ricki Lake Show* and a guest was talking about how some Christians believe God is going to end the world in 2000 because it's the millennium and there's been seven years of really bad things happening on earth. The seven years before the end is called the Tribulations and would have started back in 1993.

So if you asked Amina, she'd say we're right on track.

Except turns out when the end comes we don't all just die. The believers go up to heaven and the rest of us stay and suffer in the ruins. I'll be stuck exactly where I am, except maybe with boils or burns or radiation poisoning, with the other unbelievers including Mama and Tata and Elle and Amina, even poor senile Deda Ilić who doesn't believe in that kind of Jesus.

Mama made me get out of bed just before supper and when I turned on the TV they were advertising the *Peanuts* Christmas special for tonight, 7:00 pm Central time. Sara stayed for supper and we all sat down to watch and Mama wanted to know why all the children were behaving like petty adults and Sara told her this was an American holiday classic and she should just watch. But the thing is I thought maybe I'm getting a fever because I felt really hot and shaky watching Lucy and Charlie Brown.

In the end the dead tree miraculously comes back to life when a bunch of kids wave their hands around and give it some love because anything can happen in a cartoon.

Only that's not how life works. Maybe that's how Elle thought of me, the way Lucy thought of Charlie Brown. That's how she treated me.

Amina wrote once that *In war, everyone's hands get dirty, and civil wars are the dirtiest. But that doesn't mean some aren't guiltier than others.*

Like plenty of Bosnian Muslim a-holes and thugs did some really bad stuff once the fighting started. Or Milošević got the whole civil war rolling in the first place, but if both my parents committed suicide when I was young I'd probably have some issues too. Radovan Karadžić is another story. Amina said the bastard was a crooked psychiatrist before the war, taking bribes to declare criminals crazy so they didn't have to go to jail. Then he decides he can get some real kicks by going into politics as the Butcher of Bosnia. Need someone with no conscience to direct the Siege of Sarajevo? Order the genocide of Muslims in Srebrenica from the safety of his office? Disappear after it's all over as if he never existed as a well-known doctor or politician? Karadžić is your man!

Deda Ilić said that when Peter betrayed Jesus three times he was forgiven, but Judas, who sold out his savior for a sack of gold or something, he was another story.

I was thinking that in almost every language there's a name like Peter but you can't say that about Judas.

What I want to know is, does a guy like Milošević, who likes Disney and Frank Sinatra, does he feel guilty deep down just because most people think he is, or does he keep telling himself the same stories over and over about doing what he had to do? If you make a nightmare, commit the biggest of sins, don't the stories matter more than ever? Because if you're not the hero then you're the villain and who wants that?

Maybe it's not the big losers or big winners you have to watch out for. Amina says Hitler wanted to be a painter and Karadžić wanted to be a poet and it's the ones who think they might create something magnificent but never quite get there who end up heading on over to the Dark Side.

Tata is banging around the living room trying to straighten the Christmas tree in its stand all by himself. Turns out the son of his new Bosnian boss works in a tree lot and tucks the best ones behind the cash shed. Mama started crying because the tree is so perfect it looks artificial but with the scent of Trebevic Mountain right here in our Winnipeg apartment.

It got me thinking how even though both Mama and Tata were Tito-lovers who thought religion turned people into stupid sheep and New Year's was the only holiday worth celebrating, it was different for me because of Deda Ilić. Like I was always with him when he dragged home a big oak branch to hang over the door on Orthodox Christmas Eve. I was the only one who didn't laugh at him when he made clucking sounds while spreading straw all over Baba's polished floor because Christ wished to gather all his people in one loving community just as a hen gathers her chicks beneath her wings to keep them warm. And when Baba made money bread on Christmas Day she made sure I got the coin baked in the middle.

But I can't say the same thing about Muslim holidays. Tata never took me to Nana Spaho's on Eid al-Fitr even though I know she did the Ramadan fast all through Tito and beyond. Before the siege, Arman used to hide behind the mosque's fountain during the evening call to prayer waiting for all the street dogs to come running, howling their heads off for handouts. While the old men were prostrating inside, Arman would toss out a little scrap of mutton stolen from his mama's kitchen and we'd watch to see if any of the strays would challenge the one we called Mujo, who was really big but kind of stupid. Every once in a while Haso, a crazy little beagle with one ear would go for it and then one day Mujo didn't show up and so Haso was king.

Those scrapping dogs are what I remember most about the mosque, which when you think about it is pretty lame for a half-Muslim.

Now it's like I can't stop thinking not just about Elle, but this that and everything.

Maybe it's like with Noah Kristianson who had his Bar Mitzvah. Elle stayed home with me in solidarity because I wasn't invited and because she said Jimmy said these kinds of traditions are as archaic as cutting up a baby boy's penis. I was thinking Noah's dad was definitely not Jewish so maybe mothers call the shots when it comes to this stuff.

Like it was Mama who decided we should celebrate Christmas on the 25th and forget about Deda Ilić's clucking on January 6th. Amina said it wouldn't be fair to me because who wants birthday cake on Christmas Eve and Sara said anybody who celebrated the holidays a week or two late would look like they were *right off the boat*. Amina had to explain that one to me and she said Sara was just stirring things up.

Mama said if we were going to start fresh we should start fresh, and that was it. It's like my whole life has been women explaining things to me.

Amina just called and asked to talk to me and I said no and Tata lost it. I was in my bathrobe and Mama was still decorating the tree and humming "Bozicna pesma" and Tata grabbed my arm and pulled me into the living room and shoved the phone against my face like it was a hold-up. *For Christ's sake, are you that selfish, son? Spare a few words for your sister.*

As soon as I took the phone, he let go of me like a mugger in the movies who decides his victim isn't worth it.

Krysztof? Cris? Are you there?
Yeah.
How are you?
Okay.
No, you're not. I'm sorry, that was a stupid question. Are you still going for your sessions?
Yeah.
Have you talked to her? To Elle?
She's at her dad's.
At Jimmy's?
Yeah.
Listen, I wish I was there. I really do. You know, I made myself go to Belgrade last week and Deda Ilić thought I was Mama. Can you imagine? It's a joke how much we don't look alike. I think it's maybe the voice. We sound the same, God help me.
Yeah, you kind of sound the same.
Do you like your therapist? Is she helpful? It's a woman, right?
Yeah. She looks like a bird.
A bird? Ah, you're such a funny one. This Christmas, I don't know what to expect because things are more normal in the city all the time but everything still looks like shit. Last time I was in a taxi I tried to count the number of buildings without windows and I had to stop counting because they're all around. I feel like I know how Deda Ilić must feel, you know, being in Sarajevo. You know you're somewhere as familiar as the back of your hand but there's so much you don't recognize that you can't trust yourself.

I didn't want to cry.

Don't tell Mama, but I'm translating for the French and I met a soldier from Toulouse. They're here to repair the airport, so even if I fall for him, he'll be here for years. You get it? It's my little joke, because you have to have a dark sense of humor here, with all the European soldiers and the Swiss cheese buildings and the people who are so beaten down they don't know how to laugh anymore.

I won't tell.

Okay, well, I was just kidding, I don't care what Mama thinks. It's just the holidays and I can't sleep. I get all sentimental because it's Christmas and it's your birthday and I keep thinking of how little you were when you strutted around on stage to that Elvis song like you owned the place and now you're going to be sixteen. Do you remember that? Was it a talent show or something like that?

A talent contest.

Yeah, yeah. It was reggae, remember? My Canadian baby brother doing reggae.

You know, Amina, Elle isn't at Jimmy's. She's here. I don't know why I said that before.

Oh. Okay.

Mama said to remember it's long distance.

Tell her to mind her own business. I can afford it.

I'm pretty tired.

Oh. Okay. But when I call back in a few days you have to talk to me. Promise?

Promise.

I was crying by then, the kind of tears that slip down out of the corner of your eye, quiet as a sniper.

Time to take the pill.

December 23, 1999

Tata just banged on my door but I didn't answer and he went away. I punched the wall as hard as I could and now my first three knuckles have swollen up like ping-pong balls. The tears keep slipping and I keep wiping them away like they never existed.

I couldn't face Mama's crying so I went to see Budgie. I closed my eyes in the car because the sun was bouncing off the snow and Mama wasn't wearing any lipstick and there were suddenly all these lines in her face. I didn't think she noticed my hand until I was getting out and she said I should show it to the doctor. I told her she's not that kind of doctor and she said show her anyway.

Budgie asked me was what happening and I told her I punched the wall. She acted like everybody does that once in a while and asked how I was sleeping. I said maybe too good and she said she would adjust my prescription.

I told her I still hadn't read Elle's messages. She said I was in a lot of pain and it made sense to fend off more pain but it was time, maybe what she said would help me.

I told her I was tired of being afraid. That's why I loved Elle, because she was fearless. That's why I missed Amina.

Budgie said she didn't think anyone lives without fear. She was wearing a blue jacket with white buttons that made her look kind of businesslike only it was too small. The jacket was open and there was no way those buttons would ever be buttoned. She wanted to know why I punched the wall and I told her I didn't know. Maybe I was mad that

Amina is grown-up and I'm not. Because Amina is exactly where she's supposed to be and I'm not.

Budgie said Amina might say she doesn't care what her mama thinks but she does.

No one ever said love is easy, Laz-Aaar. It makes you care.

I asked if her daughter was sad that her parents wouldn't be together for Christmas. She cocked her head and looked confused and I pointed at her finger and she laughed like I was a baby who just did something adorable. She said she and her ex were doing most of the celebrations together, including his girlfriend, which should be fun. I asked what her daughter wanted for Christmas and she laughed again. She said Jessie was a funny kid and that she'd asked for a yellow flower and some French toast from Santa. I asked if Jessie was doing okay now that she had some help, and she said things were getting better. Then she handed me a new prescription and I said see you in 2000 and she shook my hand.

See in you 2000.

I started thinking. It's like love is the opposite of carefree. And once it happens you're stuck with it. You have to carry that care whether you like or not.

December 24, 1999

Everyone saved up and got me a PlayStation with Guardian's Crusade and Marvel Superheroes vs. Street Fighter. I can't believe it. It was Sara's idea. She also brought a cake from Jeanne's Bakery which she says is a Winnipeg institution but the bottom is a rock hard cookie and the icing is tasteless. I said Mama's war cake was better and everyone laughed except Sara who said Canadians would probably think *tulumba* was too sweet the first time they tasted it.

December 25, 1999

When Hana came over last night she asked if I wanted to give Mama a purple scarf from Sears and when Mama opened it she pretended I'd gone to the mall and picked it out myself. Guardian is a little babyish but the graphics are really good and you can pick if you want to battle. Knight has to go on this quest with his friend Nehani and they meet up with all these big heroes who think they can save the world better than anyone else. It was probably in the clearance bin because I don't think it's been a huge hit or anything.

Hana said she's going to have a baby in June and Mama is so excited I thought her head might explode. Marvel vs. Street Fighter is a sequel to the X-Men version. Ivan and I played it at the okay hotel arcade when we went to Fargo. The PS version doesn't have tag teams which isn't great, and it's your pretty standard crossover fighter. Mama said at least it's not with all the guns and prison suits and blow-ups like that Big Thief Auto, and this time Sara laughed with everyone else.

For twelve hours I've done nothing but eat and game like I'm the same as I always was. But that was only a holiday because maybe it's the same as love. Once you start thinking about things you can't put the genie back in the bottle no matter how hard you try.

Amina just called and said that in the new century they're going to try more than 100 Bosnian Serbs for crimes against humanity and the bastards are going to rot in their cells while Sarajevans rebuild every fricking spire and every fricking dome and every fricking park bench and every fricking cinema.

I asked her if she'd read Elle's messages on the computer and at first she didn't know what I was talking about. Then she laughed and said, *Why would I do that? That's your business.*

I told her I hadn't read them yet, and she laughed some more. *Oh, so you wanted me to give you hints, or maybe ease the blow? You don't need your big sisters wiping your little Canadian bum anymore because you think it's stinky. You're a big boy.*

Then she apologized and said she spent most of the day hanging out at the new hotel where all the foreigners stay, drinking too much French wine.

I told her it was okay, I was a big boy, I could take it.

But I'm not, because I still haven't read the messages.

Mama is in bed and Tata just came into my room without turning on the light and asked if I was awake. I decided not to take the pill so I was definitely not asleep. He sat at the end of my mattress and lit a cigarette like he didn't care what Mama would say. The way the smoke curled up over his head reminded me of all those times I slept on the cot in our kitchen because my bedroom was freezing and also right in the line of shelling, after the electricity cut out, listening to him chat with this or that neighbor about how close or far the shelling was.

Even in the dark I could see his face was shiny like he was running a marathon instead of talking. He said that us men, we don't talk like the women, or maybe it was just him, he didn't know. But he wanted to tell me something that he never told Mama.

I'm trying to remember, word for word.

When Baba and Deda Ilić left for Belgrade, I insisted that we stay. I believed that it wouldn't last, that the bastards could not steal such a city. But I was wrong, and as the months passed, I did the calculations. I knew with each passing day the odds turned against our family a little more. Maybe it would be your mama, or your sister, or you in the hospital with no antiseptic or antibiotics. I was frightened for you as a boy growing up to kill or be killed, and I was frightened for myself. I had trapped our family there because I was nothing more than a school math teacher. Even when the tunnel finally opened, passes out were not for people like us.

So this is what I did. I gave some powerful people some information about someone I'd known for a long time. He wasn't exactly an innocent man, but I knew his sister, his mother.

For a long time I didn't want to know about what happened to this man. I didn't want to know. And then a while back I gave Amina his name and asked her to try to find out what she could. This morning she told me she'd spoken to his sister's old hairdresser and that he'd been shot through the temple while in line for water. This means I maybe wasn't responsible for his execution. He was maybe just another victim of those men who hide behind rifle scopes, shooting what's handy.

Tata was crying but didn't seem to notice.

But you see, it doesn't matter. I still did what I did. I paid with a piece of myself, and it has left a scar that will never heal. Soon I will have a new Canadian grandbaby who won't even speak Bosnian, but for me the scar will remain.

I told him that he was a good man, that he'd saved his kids, and he sighed like I was telling him something too obvious.

I am just a man, Lazar. And I have failed you in many ways. I've not paid attention as I should.

I told him that it was okay, that I forgave him, that I was sorry too, and then he said he was going back to school in the new year to study drafting. He said math was a language he knew well and his friend was going to help him.

I told him that was good and that I wanted to go back to school too, which wasn't true, but it was a good lie and it made him smile.

And now I'm thinking about Amina's war crimes tribunal, about all the money and people and time it will take to hash over what happened for all those years to my tata's home, to face it all again so we can remember as much of the truth as we can.

And I think maybe she's right. Maybe it's worth it.

4

December 26, 1999
From: CristElle@hotmail.com
To: Spaho123@hotmail.com
Subject line: 2000

I found the pic Mindy took of us when we came in after that slushy snow fight. You're leaning into me like you want to smell my soggy hair and your eyes are closed because you are the least photogenic person that's ever lived ... and now I feel like I'm going to throw up because maybe Mindy wasn't wrong. Which is fricking rich, because what kind of straight guy prances around in matching T-shirts to the Spice Girls? I mean, into Elton John, check. Mama's boy, check. Friends with a fat chick, check. Secret crush on Ivan, check.

Like, what the hell???

I wrote to Ivan, u know. I asked him how his hair was growing back, if he'd found a band in the Emerald City, whether he thought u were a sociopath. He wrote back a nice note, said he missed Winnipeg's hidden gems like me and then he got all Dungeon-mastery. He said some people are destined to lose their way and it's not our fault or our responsibility, it's just their destiny.

And I knew he was right, like always. Everyone fricking says it. Even Amanda-P who believes in forgiveness and redemption.

Except the thing is, with Ivan sometimes I couldn't catch my breath. CristElle was never like that. I never felt lonely with u, not even when I thought u were dying. And I swear I know kind of how your tata feels now.

I don't want to fricking move on. I miss the way it was too much, even though I don't know if it ever was that way to begin with.

I just keep thinking of how we always planned to spend this New Year's … I'd have my license and we'd drive around to all the nightclubs singing karaoke and winning all the contests so we could afford our first champagne. Holy fricking shit, we were dorks on an epic scale. But the thought of CristElle driving around in Mindy's old minivan, pouring expensive bubbly into each other's mouths …

Except I keep imagining u sitting there all frizzy-headed and alone with Mama and Tata Depresso.

There is going to be a new century without CristElle. After 2000 years of bullshit, don't we deserve better than that?

December 27, 1999
From: Spaho123@hotmail.com
To: CristElle@hotmail.com
Subject line: Hi

Dear Elle … r u there? It's the day after Boxing Day.

December 27, 1999
From: CristElle@hotmail.com
To: Spaho123@hotmail.com
Subject line: re Hi

I know what day it is.

December 27, 1999
From: Spaho123@hotmail.com
To: CristElle@hotmail.com
Subject line: re Hi

I read all your messages.

December 27, 1999
From: Spaho123@hotmail.com
To: CristElle@hotmail.com
Subject line: re Hi

R u there? Can I come over?

December 27, 1999
From: CristElle@hotmail.com
To: Spaho123@hotmail.com
Subject line: re Hi

What took you so fricking long?

The Tragedy of Sarajevo for Curious Bystanders
by Amina Spaho

WHO ARE THE BALKAN SLAVS?
Most people in southeastern Europe (otherwise known as the Balkans) have a common Slav ancestry. They probably look and sound pretty much the same to you.

BUT — and this is IMPORTANT — they have lived largely different histories.

Since about the mid-1400s:

• Serbians have had ties with Orthodox Christianity and the rule of Russia.

• Croatians have had ties with Catholicism and the rule of Austria and Hungary.

• Bosnians have had ties with all of the above, plus with Islam, from when the Ottoman Turks took over for a while.

Thanks to these differences in geography, politics and religion, most of Balkan history has been filled with CLASHES AND HOSTILITY.

Except in Bosnia's capital city, Sarajevo.

Tucked in a beautiful mountain valley, Sarajevo became the place for all Slavs and their rulers — Orthodox, Catholic, Muslim — to live and trade and make their mark. In the 1500s, even Jews were welcomed when places like Spain and Portugal didn't want them.

WHAT ABOUT YUGOSLAVIA? DIDN'T ALL THE BALKANS JUST GET ALONG THEN?

It's true. After World War Two, the Balkan peoples were exhausted from all the death and destruction. They tried to overcome their centuries-old clashes.

They created one large united nation known as Yugoslavia and proclaimed Belgrade, in Serbia, its capital, led by Tito, Yugoslavia's savvy statesman and beloved leader. Tito held the Slavs together with an iron fist and Communism, an unquestioning belief in industrious team work and endless human progress.

Yugoslavia became part of the mighty Soviet Communist bloc, where differences like how or who you chose to worship, or what you could call your own, or where you felt rooted, were officially meaningless.

For fifty years, talking publicly about how Yugoslavs differed was forbidden!

YET YUGOSLAVIA LASTED ONLY 50 YEARS!

Unfortunately, Yugoslavia was bound to fail, because it turns out that how or who you choose to worship, or what you can call your own, or where you feel rooted means QUITE A BIT to most of us.

So by 1990, all the Communist bloc governments began to fall one by one.

The dying union of Yugoslavia left its young people without jobs or a future to believe in. And the age-old differences and conflicts began bubbling to the surface again like lava.

Serbs in Belgrade, who still ruled the Yugoslav Army, decided this was finally their chance to grab all the power and all the land they thought they deserved.

They went on the attack. And here's the thing. ONCE PEOPLE ARE AT WAR WITH EACH OTHER, NOTHING MATTERS BUT THEIR DIFFERENCES.

Which means havens of mixed culture like Sarajevo must be destroyed.

In 1992, Serb fighters moved into the mountains. They surrounded the citizens of Sarajevo and held the entire city under siege.

Their goal? To starve, maim and kill as many as those citizens as possible so that they would abandon their uniquely glorious city.

WHERE WAS THE REST OF THE WORLD DURING ALL THIS?
The United Nations and its alliance of Western democracies hemmed and hawed. They preferred not to get their well-manicured hands dirty in a civil war, no matter how one-sided. No matter that the JERUSALEM OF EUROPE, with its many mosques, cathedrals, onion domes and synagogues, was turning to rubble, its people dying in a rain of shrapnel and bullets.

FINALLY, with at least 10,000 already dead and 50,000 wounded, half of them CIVILIANS and CHILDREN, the world stepped up. In the fall of 1995, NATO and the UN launched Operation Deliberate Force, an air campaign that lasted less than a single month and brought the longest siege of a capital city in the history of modern warfare to an end.

Now it is a new century and Sarajevo's Bosnian War dead lie in the surrounding slopes, circling the valley.

I will not get into the fate of war criminals like the politicians Slobodan Milošević and Radovan Karadžić, or

General Ratko Mladić. You can look them up and decide for yourself if the punishments fit the crimes or, if like the historic sanctum of Sarajevo, true justice is perhaps too much to expect in this life.

With endless gratitude to my editor, Shelley Tanaka, whose careful reading and patient wisdom always made it better.

And to Dzevad Karahasan, for his sad and beautiful book, *Sarajevo, Exodus of a City* (Kodansha, 1994).

Brenda Hasiuk has published adult short stories in the *Malahat Review*, *New Quarterly* and *Prism*. She has previously written two YA novels, *Where the Rocks Say Your Name* (shortlisted for the McNally-Robinson Book of the Year and the Margaret Laurence Award for Fiction) and *Your Constant Star* (praised by *Kirkus* for its "authentic teen characters, closely observed settings and moving plot").

Brenda lives in Winnipeg, where she is on the board of Rossbrook House, an inner-city drop-in center for at-risk youth, and she heads up Project Reunite, a grassroots group working to support, settle and reunite Syrian refugee families.